# Spooksville

## Three Books in One

The Dark Corner
The Little People
The Wishing Stone

Hodder
Children's
Books

a division of Hodder Headline plc

First published in Great Britain in 1996
by Hodder Children's Books
a division of Hodder Headline plc
338 Euston Road
London NW1 3BH

This bind-up edition first published in Great Britain
by Hodder Children's Books in 1999.

A Catalogue record for this book is available from the British Library

ISBN 0 340 77335 9

Typeset by Avon Dataset Ltd, Bidford-on-Avon, Warks

Printed and bound in Great Britain by
The Guernsey Press Co. Ltd., Guernsey, Channel Islands

# Spooksville

## THE DARK CORNER

# One

It was Sally Wilcox who brought up how cool Bryce Poole was, and started the argument that led to another trip through the Secret Path. Of course later she swore she had nothing to do with what happened. It was a typical situation in Spooksville. No one ever wanted to be blamed for starting another adventure, at least not in the middle of the adventure – when it looked like they would all die.

The day started as so many did that summer. Adam Freeman, Cindy Makey, Sally Wilcox and Watch got together for a breakfast of milk and doughnuts. While stuffing their faces at the local coffee shop, they tried to figure out what to do with the day.

'Only a few weeks and we'll be back in school,' Sally said. 'We have to make the most of every day.'

'I'm kind of looking forward to going back to

school,' Cindy said. 'I like learning new things.'

'Summer vacation in Spooksville is more of a learning experience than any schooling,' Sally muttered.

'What is school like here?' Adam asked. 'Is it as weird as the rest of the town?'

'It's pretty normal,' Watch said.

'Except for a few of the teachers,' Sally added. 'Not all of them are human.'

'How did I know you were going to say that?' Cindy asked.

'We do have a couple of unusual teachers,' Watch admitted.

Sally nodded. 'There's Mr Castro. He teaches history, basically. But sometimes he talks about the future.'

'Don't say it,' Cindy interrupted. 'Mr Castro's really from the future.'

'Well, he's not from around here,' Watch said.

'I think he was built at the North Pole,' Sally said. 'If my sources are accurate.'

'I heard it was the South Pole,' Watch said.

Adam and Cindy exchanged looks. 'So he's a robot?' Adam asked.

'He's not a desktop computer,' Sally said.

Watch spoke reluctantly. 'He does seem to hav several mechanical qualities. For example, he never eats lunch. He never drinks water. When he's tired, he lies out on the football field and soaks up the sun's rays. That's how he supposedly recharges his batteries.'

'He also has a hearing aid that looks more like a cosmic receiver,' Sally said. 'He never takes it off. I hear it's wired directly into his positronic brain.' She added, 'He sure doesn't have trouble hearing.'

Cindy shook her head. 'I don't believe any of this.'

'Wait till you get him for history,' Sally said. 'And he pops his eyes out in the middle of a lecture just to clean his contact lenses.'

'You said a couple of teachers were weird,' Adam said. 'Who's the other one?'

'Mrs Fry,' Sally said. 'She teaches biology. She's a snake.'

'She has scaly skin?' Cindy asked.

'Yes,' Sally said impatiently. 'I told you, she's a snake. When have you ever seen a snake that didn't have scaly skin?'

'What Sally means is Mrs Fry seems to be part snake,' Watch said. 'She slides around the room and hisses all the time. Some people think she's a

3

descendant of a reptilian race that lived in this area millions of years ago.'

'You dissect frogs all the time in her class,' Sally said. 'But never snakes or lizards. And all the frog parts disappear between classes. She eats them all.'

Cindy made a face. 'That's gross.'

'You haven't seen gross until you've seen Mrs Fry shed her skin,' Sally said.

Adam didn't know what to make of any of this. 'It sounds like it's going to be an interesting school year.'

Sally brightened. 'There are some cute guys at school.'

Cindy was cautious. 'Are they all human?'

Sally waved her hand. 'There's this one guy, his name's Bryce Poole, and he's so cool. He's like a young James Bond. Nothing disturbs him. You'll adore him, Cindy. He's got real dark hair, and super warm brown eyes. He's only twelve but he doesn't act like a kid. He talks like a well-read sophisticated adult – like me.'

Cindy was interested. 'How come we haven't seen him this summer?'

'He's a loner,' Sally said in a confidential tone. 'He takes his own risks and he doesn't go whining to anyone about the consequences.'

'It's hard to imagine someone who's taken more

risks than us this summer,' Adam muttered.

'And I can't remember that we ever whined to anyone,' Watch added.

Sally stopped and laughed. 'Are you guys jealous of Bryce?'

Adam shrugged. 'How can I be jealous of someone I've never met?'

'I've met him and he's no big deal,' Watch said.

'What bothers you guys more?' Sally persisted. 'Is it his obvious intelligence? His smouldering looks? Or is it his dynamic attitude?'

'I told you,' Adam said. 'I've never met the guy. I know nothing about him.'

'I'm trying to tell you about him,' Sally said. 'And you're getting all upset.' She paused. 'I think you're jealous, but you don't have to be. I like him as a friend. There's nothing between us.'

'I bet he's wonderful,' Cindy gushed.

'How can you say that?' Adam demanded. 'You haven't met him either.'

'But if Cindy does fall in love with him when she meets him,' Sally said, 'you mustn't stand in her way, Adam. You have to be mature about it. So Bryce is better looking and smarter than you or Watch. It doesn't mean you're not both worthy human beings.'

'Oh boy,' Adam muttered.

'Where's a good place to meet him?' Cindy asked.

Sally spoke seriously. 'You have to catch him coming and going. He never stays in one place long. He's always taking some super risk to protect this town from danger.'

'Hold on a second,' Adam said. 'Since I've been here, what has he done to protect this town? I mean, we've had to deal with aliens, the Haunted Cave, the Cold People, not to mention the Witch. Where was he all this time?'

'Yeah,' Watch agreed. 'Bryce didn't even bother to help us out with the Howling Ghost.'

Sally smiled condescendingly. 'Bryce doesn't deal with small crises. He only handles the major ones.'

'How can you call the Cold People a small crisis?' Adam demanded. 'If we hadn't stopped them, they would have taken over the whole planet.'

'Yes, but this isn't that big a planet,' Sally said. 'Not compared to the rest of the galaxy. Bryce deals more with cosmic emergencies.'

Adam and Watch looked at each other and rolled their eyes. 'Like what?' Adam asked. 'What is this big shot Bryce doing right now to protect us?'

Sally glanced around the coffee shop to make sure

no one was listening. She spoke in a hushed tone. 'Bryce is working with the Secret Path. He's trying to halt the interdimensional flow of negativity so that it doesn't seep into our reality.'

Adam frowned. 'How do you know this?'

Sally sat back and nodded gravely. 'I have my sources.'

'I don't believe it,' Watch said. 'Bryce Poole doesn't even know what the Secret Path is. I asked him about it before talking to Bum and he didn't even know where it began.'

'He was just acting like he didn't know,' Sally said. 'He told me later after I told him about our adventures on the other side. He didn't think you were equipped enough to survive the dangers of the interdimensional portal.'

It was Watch's turn to frown. 'Equipped with what?'

'I don't want to get personal here,' Sally said.

'You are always personal,' Adam said drily.

Sally was offended. 'Don't take it out on me that Cindy is suddenly interested in another guy.'

'I didn't say that exactly,' Cindy said.

'Your voice said it all,' Sally said. 'And I understand what Adam's going through. I'm sympathetic. To experience raging jealousy and bitter rejection for the first time is not easy.'

Adam sighed. 'I am so grateful for your sympathy.'

'We're arguing about nothing,' Watch said. 'Bryce isn't a super-hero. He's probably not even using the Secret Path.'

'How do you know?' Sally shot back. 'You've been afraid to use it since that first time.'

'I haven't been afraid,' Watch said. 'I have just been busy with other things.'

'Yeah, like saving the planet with his best friend,' Adam added.

'I saved the planet too,' Sally said.

'Then you and Bryce should be perfect together,' Adam said.

Sally laughed. 'You are so jealous!'

Adam got angry. 'Why should I be jealous of a guy who thinks he's James Bond? I agree with Watch. This guy is not using the Secret Path. He doesn't have the guts.'

Sally stood. 'Why don't we go and see?'

'Go where?' Cindy asked. 'See what?'

'The Secret Path starts or ends in the cemetery,' Sally said, 'depending on how you look at it. Why don't we go there now and look for signs of Bryce? Then we can see who the real hero in this town is.'

'Why would Bryce leave signs that he's using the Secret Path?' Watch asked.

'Yeah,' Adam said. 'Who is he trying to impress?'

'You guys have an answer for everything.' Sally sniggered and turned for the door. 'Are you chickens coming or not?'

The way she worded the question, it was really impossible to say no.

# *Two*

At the cemetery they had no trouble finding Madeline Templeton's tombstone. It was larger than all the other stones, and it had a large black raven carved on the top. The bird glared down at them and Adam was reminded of the last time they had taken the path, and the horror they had experienced on the other side. He shuddered as he glanced round the cemetery. The place was dismal. The few naked trees stood like angry skeletons. A shadow seemed to hang across the dry grounds, although there wasn't a cloud in the sky.

'Did you put this here?' Watch asked Sally as he knelt by Madeline Templeton's tombstone. He held up a green knapsack. Sally took a step forward and shook her head.

'No,' she said. 'Why would I put anything here? It probably belongs to Bryce.'

'How convenient,' Adam said.

Sally ignored him. 'What does it have inside it?' she asked.

Watch opened the sack. 'Binoculars. A thermos of water. A compass. A few flares.' He held up a hunting knife. 'It looks as if Bryce was anticipating trouble.'

'But why would he leave his equipment here?' Cindy asked.

'I don't know,' Watch said.

'I don't understand something,' Cindy said. 'How do you get through this Secret Path? You guys said something about walking backwards into the tombstone?'

'It's not that easy,' Adam explained. 'First you have to trace a route all over Spooksville. Then you have to walk from the front gate of the cemetery backwards into the tombstone.'

'Can't you just walk backwards into the tombstone,' Cindy asked, 'and forget the other stuff?'

'No,' Watch said. 'I tried it once not long ago and it didn't work. First you have to visit the location of each of the significant events in Madeline Templeton's life. You have to go to each place in order. Somehow that opens the portal to other dimensions.'

'Then Bryce must have done that?' Cindy asked.

12

'I'm not convinced this stuff belongs to Bryce,' Adam interrupted. 'It doesn't have his name on it.'

'You simply refuse to accept the fact that he is using the Secret Path,' Sally said.

'What are we arguing about here?' Watch said, before another argument could break out. 'It's possible Bryce is using the Secret Path. I admit that much now. But so what? What does it have to do with us?'

'Nothing,' Sally said simply. 'I was merely trying to make the point that Bryce is braver than you guys.'

'Oh boy,' Adam muttered.

'Well you haven't gone back through the path,' Sally said. 'But he has, many times.'

'The Secret Path is dangerous,' Adam said. 'If he's dumb enough to keep using it, then that's his problem.'

'It is only dangerous if you're not strong enough to handle it,' Sally said.

'I can't believe you just said that,' Adam said. 'You were the one who was against us using it in the first place.'

'Wait a second,' Watch said. 'Sally does have a point. Remember what Bum told us when he spoke about the path. He said, "The Secret Path doesn't always lead to the same place. It all depends on you. If you're a little scared, you end up in a place that's a little scary. If you're terrified, the path is like a road to terror." '

'I'm sure Bryce is able to control his fear,' Sally said. 'And go where he wishes.'

'Good for him,' Adam said sarcastically.

'I'm not saying you should follow him,' Sally said.

'We don't have to do that,' Watch agreed.

'I mean, you don't have to try to impress me,' Sally said. 'I like you guys the way you are. I don't care how brave you are. Do you care, Cindy?'

'No,' Cindy replied. But then she considered. 'But I would like to meet this guy.'

'He's a real hero,' Sally said.

Adam and Watch looked at each other and it would be safe to say they each looked pretty disgusted.

'Do you feel like she's trying to push us on to the path again?' Adam asked.

'It feels like it,' Watch said.

'Why do you think?' Adam asked, ignoring the girls for a moment.

'I think, personally, that she's worried Bryce is trapped on the other side of the Secret Path,' Watch said. 'I think she wants us to go and rescue him, but she's too proud to say it outright.'

'My thoughts exactly,' Adam said.

Sally didn't protest. They had hit a nerve with her. For a moment she stared at the wicked tombstone, then she lowered her head.

'He's been gone a while,' she said finally.

'How do you know?' Cindy asked.

'He told me he was going,' Sally said quietly. 'That was a week ago. I haven't seen him since.'

'Is this his knapsack?' Watch asked. 'Why did he leave it on this side?'

Sally shrugged. 'I think it's his. I don't know why he didn't take it with him.'

'Why was he using the path?' Adam asked.

'I told you the truth on that point,' Sally said. 'He said he had to stop the overflow of evil into our dimension.'

'At least he sets his sights high,' Adam remarked.

'If we're going to use the Secret Path, we have to start now,' Watch said, checking one of his four watches, which he always wore. 'It takes half the day to visit all the important places in Madeline Templeton's life.'

'Wait a second,' Adam said. 'Before we go to all that trouble we have to decide if we even *can* help Bryce. There's no reason to think if we step through the path we'll end up in the same dimension as him. We might end up back where we were last time, and that's one place I don't want to see again.'

'But if he is trapped,' Sally said, 'how can you just leave him to an eternity of torment and agony?'

'Better him than us,' Watch said wisely.

Adam put his hand on Sally's shoulder. 'You're really worried about him, aren't you? That was just a show at the coffee shop, wasn't it? You've been trying to bully us into taking the path.'

Sally nodded. 'He's never been gone this long before. I'll go with you guys if you go.' She paused. 'I'm not afraid.'

'Yeah, you are,' Watch said. 'We're all afraid to try the path again, and we can't just talk ourselves out of our fear. And that means if we do take it, we'll probably end up in a scary place.'

Sally nodded as she stared up at the tombstone. 'In an evil place, where Bryce went.'

# *Three*

The sequence they had taken before to get on to the
Secret Path had been:

1 The beach (where Madeline was supposedly
   born).
2 Derby Tree (where Madeline cursed the tree and
   turned its leaves red).
3 A cave (where Madeline killed a lion with her
   bare hands).
4 The chapel (where Madeline got married).
5 The reservoir (where Madeline drowned her
   husband).
6 The beach (where Madeline was almost burned to
   death).
7 The cemetery (where Madeline was buried).

Obviously going to the beach twice seemed stupid, but the sequence, they knew, was the key. Going to the cave and then to the chapel and then back to the reservoir was also inconvenient, since the caves were not far from the reservoir. But they stuck to what they had done before because it had worked.

It was close to four o'clock by the time they got back to the cemetery. Starting at the front gate, they began to walk backwards towards the tombstone, holding hands.

'Why do we have to do this?' Cindy asked, sounding nervous.

'Because Madeline Templeton was carried here upside down,' Adam said. 'This is our symbolic way of re-enacting that event.' He paused. 'You sound scared.'

'I am scared,' Cindy said quickly. 'I've never gone through an interdimensional portal before.'

'We're really going to end up in a horrible place,' Sally muttered.

'Maybe you shouldn't go with us,' Adam said to Cindy. 'You could stand guard on this side.'

'What am I guarding?' Cindy asked, sounding interested.

'You never know what might come back through the portal,' Sally said.

'It might be a good idea if one of us does stay on this

side,' Watch said. 'If we don't return, that person could go for help.' He added, 'I don't mind standing guard.'

Sally glanced over her shoulder at the approaching tombstone. 'I bet none of us would mind staying at this point.' But then she suddenly let go of Cindy's hand. 'But it should be Cindy. The rest of us are experienced with this portal.'

'Are you guys sure?' Cindy asked, also letting go of Adam's hand, watching them as they continued to trudge backwards towards the grave. 'I don't mind staying behind.'

'You're the logical choice to stay,' Adam said, trying to reassure her. 'There's no use going through the portal if you don't want to do it.'

'Like we're all having a barrel of fun here,' Sally remarked.

Cindy walked beside them as they stumbled backwards. 'I feel like a coward.'

'You should,' Sally said. 'But I'll try not to bother you about it.' She paused. 'If Bryce should reappear before we do, send him looking for us.'

'Have him bring his knife,' Watch said.

'No,' Adam said. 'Cindy, grab the knapsack. I want to bring his stuff with us.'

Cindy hurried to the tombstone and grabbed the

bag. She handed it to Adam as the gang neared the wall of stone.

'How long should I wait here before I go for help?' she asked.

'If we're not back by dark,' Watch said, 'find Bum, tell him what's happened. He might be able to help.'

'If he can be bothered,' Sally added.

'We're just about there,' Adam said anxiously. 'Let's hold on to each other tightly. Goodbye, Cindy. Wish us luck.'

'Good luck!' Cindy called.

'I feel a whole lot better now that she's blessed us,' Sally said.

They stumbled as they stepped on to the grave site. For a moment Adam thought they would fall on to the Secret Path. Suddenly everything went black and he felt as if he was sinking fast. His friends seemed many miles away. He couldn't see them. He was in the eye of a hurricane, where everything was perfectly calm, for the moment, although he knew madness raged all around him.

# *Four*

When everything returned to normal Adam realised they were in a place that was far from normal. It was Spooksville and it was not. As they looked round in wonder, they realised they were in the heavenly counterpart of home. A sweet scent filled the air. The surrounding trees were a lush green. Everything seemed to be glowing with a faint golden light, radiating love and joy.

'This isn't so bad,' Sally remarked.

'It looks like paradise,' Watch said, removing his glasses to clean them. 'It's amazing we came to such a nice place, what with how scared we all were.'

'I wasn't scared,' Sally said quickly, letting go of their hands. 'I think it was me who lifted our overall vibes.'

'I like how your arms shake so much when you're not scared,' Adam said.

'They only shook because they were holding on to your arms,' Sally said, stepping away from the tombstone. She sucked in a deep breath of the sweet air. 'I love this place! Look at that sky. It looks like one huge rainbow. I don't know if I want to go home.'

Watch was concerned. 'We tried the Secret Path for a purpose, to find Bryce. But if he's off fighting evil, I doubt he's here.'

'That's true,' Adam agreed. Then he stopped and stared down at some initials on the bottom of the tombstone – BP. He pointed them out to the others. 'Bryce Poole. He must have been here.'

Sally bent over the initials. 'It's only a couple of letters, but it looks like his handwriting.' She raised her head and stared out of the cemetery, which actually looked more like a park. 'I wonder where he could have gone?'

'We could walk into town and ask for him,' Watch said, still fiddling with his glasses. 'I think I see people in the distance.'

'Wait a second,' Adam said. 'We should figure out where we are before we talk to anyone.'

'That's easy,' Sally said. 'We're in heaven.'

'You mean we're in *a* heaven,' Adam said. 'This place is beautiful but it's still Spooksville. See, the castle's over there, and the same ocean is down that way.'

'What I mean is we don't have to worry about getting killed here,' Sally said. 'I think if Bryce is around, people will be happy to lead us to him.'

'Then why did he carve his initials on the bottom of the tombstone?' Adam said. 'He could have just set out a sign announcing that he was here.'

'He might have been afraid of something,' Watch agreed.

Sally laughed. 'Nonsense! This is one place I'm not afraid of. Let's go and explore. I think Bryce is here, and that when we find him he'll probably be having the time of his life.'

'I hope you're right,' Adam said.

They got on to the road that wound down towards the sea and the centre of town. Along the way they passed the castle. To their immense surprise they saw Ms Ann Templeton – or at least this dimension's counterpart – supervising a picnic for a bunch of dwarves and elves. She waved as they looked over, and they didn't know what else to do so they waved back. They seemed to be having a barbecue of chicken and fish. Each of the dwarves had a can of Coke in hand, but the elves were all drinking orange soda out of clear glass bottles.

'See,' Sally said. 'Here she doesn't have any of those nasty goblins working for her.'

'I kind of liked Belfart,' Watch mused. 'I hope the Marines accepted him.'

'Maybe we should stop and talk to Ann Templeton,' Adam wondered aloud. 'Get the lowdown on this place.'

'No,' Sally said. 'I want to get into town. Bryce is most likely there.' She added, 'I wouldn't mind going to my house, and seeing what the Sally on this side is like.'

'I don't know if that would be a good idea,' Adam said, although the same thought had occurred to him. 'It might complicate things if we meet ourselves.'

'It might give us a mild case of schizophrenia,' Watch agreed.

'You guys are no fun today,' Sally said. 'I'm dying to meet the heavenly version of myself – no pun intended. I bet I'm simply extraordinary.'

'There is a lot of room for improvement,' Adam muttered.

Sally snorted. 'I heard that. Come on, let's at least get something to eat. I bet the food here is delicious.'

They ended up stopping at a fast food joint on the edge of town. In their normal Spooksville the place was called Fred's Fat Food. But here the place was called Friend's Fantastic Food. Plus the guy at the counter didn't look anything like the original Fred, who had tattoos on his arms and dirty fingernails and an apron stained with human blood. The handsome young man who took their order had long golden locks and eyes as bright blue as the clear sky. In fact, he didn't even want to be paid. He pushed their money back when they set it on the counter. The food was on the house.

'I could get into living here,' Sally said.

'Maybe that's why Bryce didn't return,' Watch said. 'He liked it so much he just decided to stay.'

'Whatever he decided we have to go back,' Adam said. 'Cindy's waiting for us. She'll start to get worried.'

'If she hadn't been such a coward she could be with us here now,' Sally said.

'You thought she should stay,' Adam protested.

'And I'm glad she did,' Sally said. 'She was so scared – we probably all would have ended up in some dark corner of the universe.'

Their food arrived and it was divine. Really, it tasted better than any meal they'd ever had in their lives, and it was just three hot-dogs and chips. Sally was so pleased by the food that she ordered a vanilla milk-shake as well, which she refused to share with Adam.

'You can still get fat in heaven,' she said. 'I wouldn't want that for you if we're going to live forever now.'

When they were about to leave the place, Adam struck up a conversation with the young man who served them. He listened patiently while Adam explained how they were searching for a friend named Bryce Poole. Adam even asked Sally to describe Bryce. When they had finished the man said in a sympathetic tone:

'You three are not from round here, are you?'

'Not exactly,' Adam replied. 'We're sort of from a neighbouring city, if you know what I mean.'

The man nodded. 'I understand. We get people like you now and then.'

'You do?' Sally asked, amazed.

'Yes,' the young man said. 'And the best thing you can do, no matter what the situation, is go find your counterpart in the city. Once you find him or her, everything will be all right.'

'That's exactly what I wanted to do,' Sally said, looking rather pleased with herself.

Watch was confused. 'So you know we're not from this dimension?'

The young man with the golden hair smiled. 'That's obvious to all of us.'

'You mean everyone in the city knows we're strangers here?' Adam asked.

The man ignored the question. 'Find your counterpart and everything will become clear.' He paused and stared off into the distance. As he did so a strange light shone in his eyes. 'I think they're waiting for you at Adam's house.'

'Waiting for us?' Watch asked. 'How do they know we're here?'

The man just smiled again. 'You'd better hurry. You don't want to keep them waiting.'

Feeling confused, Adam left the food place with his friends. Sally was insistent they head straight for Adam's house. But both Watch and Adam were having doubts.

'He didn't really answer our questions,' Watch complained.

'He said our other selves would help us,' Sally replied. 'He was a nice man – we can trust him.'

'He seemed like a nice man,' Adam said. 'But I agree with Watch. He gave vague answers.'

'I don't care what you guys say,' Sally replied. 'I'm going to see my better half. I can hardly wait to have a deep conversation with her.'

'That's one argument she's finally going to lose,' Watch said.

Since they didn't know exactly what was bothering them, Adam and Watch reluctantly agreed to accompany Sally to visit their other halves. Finding Adam's house was not difficult. It was exactly where it was in the other Spooksville.

Their three counterparts were sitting outside Adam's house.

They smiled when they saw them.

All six of them smiled.

Then the counterparts stood and walked towards them.

As they did so, their faces began to change.

They began to melt. Into hideous demon forms.

# *Five*

It was too late. The three demons – they even had horns now – were on them in an instant. Adam was struck across the face with a scaly hand. His arms were yanked behind his back. He felt a sharp pain in his spine and dropped Bryce Poole's knapsack. For a moment everything went black and he thought he would pass out. Then he realised he was being dragged towards a steel pole, which he had not noticed a second ago. It stood in the centre of his garden, spiked chains hanging from its side.

The garden was no longer the same. All round them the scenery was changing, becoming darker and dirtier, lit with a chilling red glow. It was as if the heavenly version of Spooksville was turning into a hellish realm. The demon that had hold of Adam leered in his face. The creature's teeth were sharp, his eyes like those of a wicked cat, green and splintered with thick red veins. The nails on his claws were like razors. He hissed at Adam.

'We have you now, fool!' the demon said as he snapped Adam's wrists into cuffs attached to the chains. Beside him, Adam saw the same torture happening to Watch and Sally. Each had a demon on them, leering in their face. Adam's demon giggled, 'You're never going to escape!'

Adam fought to remain calm. 'Who are you? What is this place?' The town continued to change into a nightmare realm of ruined buildings and howling creatures. Up and down the street Adam could see there were many poles where poor people had been chained. Most hung lifeless, little more than skeletons, but a few still struggled to break free. The demon tugged at Adam's hair and slobbered on his shirt.

'Who am I?' the demon asked. 'I am you. I am your dark half. And this place is the Dark Corner. Those who come here from your world never return.'

'But everything looked so nice at first,' Adam said.

The demon howled. 'We always put on a show for newcomers! You humans are so stupid!'

Adam tried to sound brave, although he was in reality terrified. Most of the other prisoners he could see looked as if they had been here for ages.

'What are you going to do with us?' he demanded.

'Let you rot here until the Gatekeepers come to judge you,' the demon said. He yanked hard on Adam's head, pulling out a clump of hair. He held it up for Adam and the others to see. 'With this I can enter your world, and be you! My partners and I will pass through the Secret Path and ruin everything that is yours!'

'No!' Adam pleaded. 'Wait! We can talk about this!'

But the demon was not listening. With his partners – who had also torn off locks of hair from Watch and Sally – he put the hair in his mouth and slowly chewed it down. Then, as if by some wicked miracle, he began to change back into the form he had when they first saw him. Now he looked like Adam, and the other two demons once again resembled Watch and Sally.

'Now we have a piece of you inside us!' Adam's demon sneered. 'We're free to go where we wish!'

'You can't go into our world!' Sally shouted at the demons. 'You'll never get away with it! Our friends will spot you immediately, and you'll be destroyed.'

Adam's demon laughed in her face. 'By the time your friends know who we are they will be here with you! Rotting in the Dark Corner!'

'But maybe we can work out a compromise,' Watch

suggested. 'I can see why you don't like living here. It's a nasty place. We have ghettos back in our world that are like this. Maybe we can help you find a better place to live, and you can let us go.'

The demons howled with delight. 'We don't want to let you go!' Adam's demon said. 'We love it when humans suffer! We live for suffering! Come, my pals, let's go and play with these fools' friends!'

Adam and the others tried to stop them, but the demons danced away, heading in the direction of the cemetery and the interdimensional portal. Adam had never felt so miserable in his whole life as he did right then. It was not as if his wrists were simply chained. They were pinned above his head, and the spikes in his cuffs were digging into his skin. Of course, Watch and Sally were in equally uncomfortable positions. All round them the air filled with fumes and ash. It was difficult to breathe. Adam coughed as his throat dried. Sally hung her head as if she was about to weep.

'I'm sorry,' she said. 'It just seemed like such a nice place.'

'The demons made it seem that way so that we would drop our guard,' Adam said grimly. 'But don't blame yourself. We were fooled as well.'

'But we probably wouldn't be in this situation if it wasn't for you,' Watch added.

'That is true,' Adam had to admit.

Sally moaned. 'I said I'm sorry. What else am I supposed to do?'

'If you could reach Bryce's knapsack, we might be able to use the knife to pick these locks,' Watch suggested. It was closest to Sally. 'See if you can catch the strap with your foot.'

'I'll try,' Sally said as she strained with her right foot towards the bag. Just another few centimetres and she would have been able to reach it, but even arching her back and kicking out, the tip of her shoe kept missing the straps. After a couple of minutes of struggling she gave up. She sighed. 'I can't do it. What are we going to do now?'

'Probably rot for eternity,' Watch said.

'Don't say that,' Adam said. 'We have to maintain a positive attitude.'

'I don't know if a positive attitude helps when you're in hell,' Sally mumbled.

'We're not in hell,' Adam said. 'We're in *a* hell. That's not exactly the same thing.'

Sally stared down the street at the other captured people. A few moaned in pain. A couple even had bird's nests on top of their heads. The black ravens croaked in their dry hair. Sally sighed again.

'Right now I don't think it makes much difference,' she said.

'Look,' Adam said, trying to sound upbeat. 'We've been in difficult situations before and we've always managed to find our way out. We'll do the same this time. We just have to come up with a plan of escape.'

'We're waiting,' Watch said.

'Well,' Adam said. 'First we have to break out of these chains. Let's concentrate on that.'

'I don't think the power of our concentration is going to break these chains,' Sally said.

'I can't believe you guys are ready to give up,' Adam complained.

Watch nodded down the street. 'It looks like a tall demon is coming. I hope it's not one of those Gatekeepers the others mentioned. They didn't sound all that friendly.'

Watch was right. Another monster was approaching.

# Six

'I don't know if I can go out tonight,' Cindy said. 'I think my mother wants me to stay in and babysit my little brother.'

'We'll take him with us as well,' Sally said, stepping forward. 'Enough talk. We want to go to town. We have much to do.'

'OK,' Cindy said, puzzled by their rude attitude. 'We can go back to town. Where would you like to go?'

'We need food,' Watch said. 'We need meat.'

'Do you want to go to Harry's Hamburgers?' Cindy asked.

'Yeah, let's go and get Harry!' Adam squealed.

'Let's go eat Harry!' Sally yelled.

'Eat his meat!' Watch joined in.

Cindy forced a smile. 'You guys must be really hungry.'

At Harry's her friends continued their odd behaviour. They ordered two hamburgers each, nothing else, not even drinks. Then they stopped Harry before he had begun to cook the food.

'We like our meat rare,' Adam said.

'We like it raw,' Sally added, as she grabbed one of the uncooked hamburgers and stuffed it into her mouth. In four huge bites she had eaten the whole thing. Cindy stared in amazement. Sally had not even chewed the food. She was eating as if she was, why, an animal. Cindy sat down at one of the tables and shook her head.

'What happened to you guys on the other side of the Secret Path?' she asked.

They all grinned. 'We had fun,' Adam said. 'That's all. Don't you believe us?'

'No, I don't,' Cindy said. 'Something happened to you over there. Tell me what it was.'

'What if we don't want to tell you?' Sally asked in a deadly tone.

'I don't know,' Cindy said, getting nervous. 'I'll do something. I'll talk to Bum.'

Watch came and sat by Cindy's side. He put his hand on her shoulder. He spoke with a big bite of uncooked hamburger in his mouth.

'You had better not talk about us,' he said. 'We get mad when people do that. We get very mad and then we do *things*.'

Cindy stared at him, stricken. 'What do you mean? What kind of *things?*'

Watch leaned closer. 'Horrible things,' he said softly.

Cindy's mouth quivered. 'Watch,' she said, 'what's wrong with you. You never talk this way.'

'He's talking just fine,' Sally said as she came and sat on Cindy's other side. She put a hand on Cindy's bare leg and Cindy felt as if she was being touched by a lizard. Sally stared at her with strangely bloodshot eyes. Cindy wanted to look away but found she couldn't. For a moment it seemed there was only Sally's eyes, eyes that didn't really belong to a young girl at all. It seemed that the pupils of Sally's eyes were really stone windows, that opened into a place of fire and pain. They bore into Cindy's brain, and Sally leaned over and whispered in her ear. Cindy noticed then how cold her breath was, and how it stank, just faintly, of a smell Cindy could not identify.

Out of the corner of her eye Cindy saw Adam

approach Harry, who had come around the counter, curious as to what they were up to. But Harry didn't actually make it all the way around the counter. There was a swift movement and then it seemed as if Harry sat down. Or maybe it was that he fell over, Cindy could not be sure. Suddenly she was unsure of most things. Sally spoke in her brain more than in her ear.

'We are normal,' Sally whispered. 'We are the way we have always been. You are not to talk to anyone about us. If you do talk about us, you will feel pain. We will make you feel pain.'

'Yes,' Cindy whispered back, as if from far away. A portion of her knew that her friends – if they were her friends – were trying to hypnotise her. But she lacked the will to resist. She did manage to turn her head slightly, however, away from Sally. But she just ended up staring into Adam's eyes, who now stood directly in front of her. His eyes were worse than Sally's, if that was possible. They seemed to burn with hateful red flames. He leaned close as she struggled to close her own eyes.

'You have no power to resist us,' he said in a cruel voice. 'You are under our control. You will go home now and act as if nothing has happened. But later tonight we will come for you, and take you and your little brother away.' He grinned and his mouth was full of many sharp teeth. 'We will take you to the Dark Corner.'

# Seven

The demon that approached Adam, Sally and Watch was taller than the others had been, and thinner. He was also dressed differently. He wore a grey cloak instead of a furry hide, and he walked more like a man than a demon. The demons had seemed to dance and jump around like hungry animals. This demon headed straight for them as if he had important business to complete. Adam had no doubt that he was one of the dreaded Gatekeepers, and that he would soon judge them and then torture them to his heart's content.

The gang looked anxiously at each other as the demon drew near.

'Maybe we can reason with him,' Sally said.

'Like we reasoned with the others?' Watch said.

'Whatever happens,' Sally said, 'I don't want to go

first. And don't tell him it was my idea we came to this horrible place.'

'Go first with what?' Adam asked.

'With whatever he's going to do to us,' Sally said.

'Don't worry,' Watch said. 'He'll probably lower us into the boiling pit together.'

'Shh,' Adam said. 'He's almost here. Don't give him any ideas.'

The demon arrived a minute later. He stood directly in front of them and studied them up and down. His face was as ugly as the other demons, with scaly skin, a wide slobbering mouth, and piercing green eyes. He scanned up and down the street, then it seemed as if he whispered to himself.

The whispers sounded vaguely human.

'What are you three doing here?' he asked, keeping his head down.

'It wasn't my idea to come,' Sally said quickly.

'We mean you no harm,' Adam said. 'We are here looking for a friend.'

'What is this friend's name?' the demon asked.

Adam squirmed against the pole that held him bound. 'His name is not important,' he said. 'At least not to you. He's our friend. We only want to find him and leave this place.'

'Your counterparts have stolen a lock of your hair?' the demon asked.

'Yes,' Watch said.

'Then it is not easy to leave here,' the demon said. 'They have probably crossed over to your world by now. You cannot return until they decide to return here.' He paused. 'Or until they are forced to return here.'

Adam wondered at all the information the demon was volunteering. 'Who are you? Are you a Gatekeeper?'

The demon spoke in a whisper. 'I am not a Gatekeeper. But one will soon come for you. You must not let him take you. If he does, you are doomed. You will never escape from here.'

'You speak like a friend,' Watch said. 'Are you here to help us?'

The demon nodded. 'I am here to help.' As he spoke he reached up and peeled back his face, and they saw that he only wore a demon's mask. In the sober red light of the hellish realm a handsome young boy with dark hair and brown eyes stared at them.

'Bryce!' Sally exclaimed. 'I knew we would find you!'

Bryce put his finger to his lips and glanced once more up and down the street. 'Shh! Don't say my name so loudly. I am a hunted man.'

'But you're only a kid like us,' Watch said.

'Here I am a great danger to the Gatekeepers' power,' Bryce said firmly. 'I have been here almost a year, fighting their powers of darkness.'

'But I saw you last week,' Sally said.

'Time moves differently in the Dark Corner,' Bryce said. 'This is a place of pain. There is so much suffering – time passes at a crawl.'

'It's moving pretty slowly for us right now, chained here,' Watch said, trying to stretch his arms. 'Can you loosen these cuffs?'

Bryce nodded and picked up his knapsack. 'It is lucky you brought my knife and other supplies. I will be able to pick your locks.'

'Why did you leave your knapsack on the other side of the Secret Path?' Adam asked.

'I have left supplies at a dozen different portals along the Secret Path,' Bryce said, taking the knife and working on Sally's cuffs. 'I came here with another knapsack, but have since had to trade my supplies to get this disguise.'

'Who traded with you?' Adam asked.

Bryce spoke in a hushed tone. 'There are many creatures in the Dark Corner who hate the Gate-keepers. They are willing to help you, a little, if you give them something in return. But they're all scared, even the best of them. They will not risk their lives to help me escape from here.' Sally's cuffs popped open. 'That's why I need your help.'

'Was it true what you said?' Adam asked. 'That we cannot return to our world until the other demons return here?'

Bryce was grim. 'That is the rule. And none of your demons will willingly return here. They will stay in the real Spooksville as long as they can.'

'But then we're trapped here forever,' Sally moaned.

'No,' Bryce said. 'I was not tricked like you were when I first arrived here. Everyone told me to go and see my counterpart, but that just made me suspicious. I hid and tried to learn how things work here. Then I finally saw someone meet their counterpart, and I saw how the world changed after the illusion had served its purpose.' Bryce nodded down the street. 'That poor soul is chained over there. He has already been judged by the Gatekeepers, and condemned to an eternity of rotting on a steel pole.'

'Do the Gatekeepers ever let anyone go?' Watch asked.

'Rarely,' Bryce said. 'You have to be a saint to escape their judgment.' He finished opening Watch's cuffs and turned to Adam. 'My counterpart knows I'm here. He searches for me everywhere. But as long as I don't touch him, I'm safe.'

'But if he hasn't got you, can't you just leave here?' Adam asked.

Bryce shook his head. 'It's not that simple. I need my counterpart to open the Secret Path for me. That's the way it is in the Dark Corner. There is no easy way out. But I cannot drag my counterpart to the tomb. You saw how strong they are. He would just overpower me, and steal a lock of my hair, and escape to our world as your counterparts have done.'

'What are they doing in our world?' Adam asked, anxious to be free of the cuffs. Already his arms were aching.

Bryce looked worried. 'They cause pain wherever they go. It is their nature. Tell me, did you leave anyone guarding the other side of the tombstone?'

'Cindy Makey is waiting for us there,' Sally said. 'You know her, Bryce. She's that homely girl who moved here a few weeks ago.'

'She's actually very nice looking,' Adam said.

Bryce nodded. 'I know her. We must assume the worst, that the demons have already got to her.' He snapped Adam's cuffs free.

46

'Thanks,' Adam said. 'What will they do to her?'

'First they will try to control her mind,' Bryce said. 'Then they will bring her here, to be judged by the Gatekeepers. They will try to bring as many as possible here. They will force them through the Secret Path. They're demons – they don't have to hike all over our city to open it.'

'What can we do?' Sally asked.

'You must help me catch my own counterpart,' Bryce said. 'Remember, I can't touch him. You must over-power him and drag him to the tombstone. If his hand touches the stone, that will be enough to open the portal for me. Once I'm on the other side, I'll deal with your demons.'

'How do we know you won't just leave us here?' Watch asked.

'Watch!' Sally exclaimed. 'How can you ask such a thing. Bryce is a hero.' She paused and added, 'You really will come back for us, won't you, Bryce?'

'Yes. But I can't promise that I will be able to handle all of your demons. I can only do the best I can.' He glanced up at the sky. 'Come, it's getting dark. If you think this place is bad now wait until later. All the demons run wild at night, and they're starving. They love nothing more than to skin a human and eat him alive.'

'Sounds like a party,' Sally muttered sarcastically.

Cindy was lying in the grass by Madeline Templeton's tombstone when the others reappeared. Because she was resting with her eyes closed, she heard them before she saw them. She was surprised. They had only been gone a few minutes. She sat up when she heard them talking. They stood huddled together in front of the tombstone.

'You guys just left.' She was so relieved to see them again she broke into a huge grin. 'Did you find Bryce?'

They paused and stared at each other, as if surprised by her question. Then Adam said in a flat voice, 'We weren't looking for Bryce.'

Cindy got up slowly. 'But that's why you used the Secret Path. We talked about it before you left. Don't you remember, Sally?'

Sally broke into a smile at being addressed. She was looking round as if she had never seen the cemetery before. 'We didn't find him,' she said in a rather heavy voice. 'But it doesn't matter. We don't need him.'

Cindy was confused. 'But you were worried about him.'

'He's gone,' Watch said simply. 'He's not a problem. Take us to town.'

'What did you see on the other side of the tombstone?' Cindy asked. 'Anything exciting?'

For a moment their eyes seemed to brighten. Indeed, it was as if a faint red light shone in them. Cindy blinked her own eyes, thinking she must have imagined it.

'Would you like us to show you what we saw?' Sally asked.

Cindy shrugged. 'Yeah. If it's safe.'

Adam turned to Sally. 'We're not showing her anything right now. We have things to do here first. Later we will take her.'

'Where will you take me?' Cindy asked.

Adam smiled strangely. 'To a nice place. We will take you there tonight.'

# *Eight*

Bryce knew where his own personal demon was. It seemed the monster was fond of hanging out at the beach. As they crept round the boulders of the jetty, they spotted him digging in the sand, searching for tiny crabs. When he would find one he would pop it in his mouth and swallow without chewing. He wouldn't even bother washing off the sand. He was an ugly little runt, but once again Bryce warned them all how strong he was.

'We can't take him by force,' Bryce said. 'Even the three of you could not handle him in his normal demonic state. You would end up all bitten and bleeding and he would just get away.'

'Do demons have a weak spot?' Watch asked.

'Yes,' Bryce said. 'They're sensitive to the cold. Notice how he doesn't actually let the water touch him, and this water is much warmer than the water at home. Cold slows them down. They're used to all the hellish fires here. What I'm going to do right now is fetch a glass of cold red lemonade. I know a place nearby where I can get it. Then one of you is going to walk by and offer it to him. Tell him that it's a glass of human blood. A demon can't resist blood. He'll gulp it down before he realises how cold it is. That should knock him out, or at least make him easier to handle.'

'How come you haven't tried this before?' Watch asked suspiciously.

'You know the answer to that,' Bryce said. 'I can't get near him. He'll recognise me. But he won't recognise any of you, not if you wear my mask and robe.'

'I'll give him the drink if the boys are too afraid,' Sally said. 'I trust you, Bryce. Did you know it was me who wanted to rescue you?'

'That's not what she wanted to tell the Gatekeeper,' Adam muttered.

Bryce wasn't interested in their group arguments. He warned them to keep his demon in sight, and keep their heads down, then he disappeared. Watch and Adam exchanged doubtful looks.

'I don't know if I trust this guy,' Watch said.

'I know what you mean,' Adam said. 'But I don't know if we have much choice.'

'What is wrong with you?' Sally demanded. 'Bryce is the salt of the earth. He rescued us once already. You should be grateful.'

'He rescued us so that we could rescue him,' Watch said. 'Once he disappears through the Secret Path we have no guarantee he's going to come back for us.'

'He himself said he's been here a year,' Adam told Sally. 'That's a long time in this kind of place. It must have changed him somehow. He might not be the same Bryce you said goodbye to last week.'

Sally was annoyed. 'Bryce is strong, inside and out. If anyone could survive here, it's him. What are you saying anyway? That he's in league with the Gatekeepers?'

'It's a possibility,' Watch said. 'The moment he's through the portal, they might jump on us.'

'Maybe he's worked out some kind of deal with them,' Adam agreed.

'Nothing changes,' Sally growled. 'You guys are jealous of him because he's so cool and competent.'

'We'll see how competent he is if he manages to get our demons back through the portal,' Watch said.

Adam sighed. 'I hope they haven't been too rough on Cindy.'

'I think the demons will be a good influence on her,' Sally said. 'Cindy needs a few rough edges to give her more personality.'

Bryce returned ten minutes later. In his hand he had a dirty glass of ice cold red lemonade. He held it out for Sally to take but now she seemed doubtful.

'How can your demon be so stupid to think a glass of lemonade is a glass of blood?' she asked.

'Demons as a whole are pretty stupid,' Bryce said. 'That's the only reason I've been able to survive here as long as I have.'

'But what if the demon only drinks a little of the lemonade?' Adam asked. 'Just enough to make him mad? He could attack Sally and hurt her.' He paused. 'I should go in her place.'

'I don't care which one of you goes,' Bryce said. 'I just need to knock this guy out as soon as possible. Remember you've got three demons running around Spooksville right now.'

'Give me your costume,' Adam said. 'Let's get this over with.'

Adam donned Bryce's demon suit and took the glass of cold lemonade. Trying to act like a normal demon out for an evening stroll, Adam walked in the direction of Bryce's demon. The monster looked up before he was halfway to him.

'Hi,' Adam called. 'Caught any good-tasting crabs?'

The demon snorted and slowly stood. He eyed Adam suspiciously. Adam was not as big as Bryce. The disguise didn't fit quite as well as it should have.

'What do you want?' the demon demanded.

'A whole bunch of human kids came through the Secret Path today,' Adam said. 'You probably heard about them. We've been over with the Gatekeepers drinking their blood. I have a glass here if you want it. I'm stuffed – I don't think I could get another drop down.'

The demon took a step closer and stared at the glass. 'Is it fresh blood?'

'Sure. Just drained it out of the fat kid myself. Have a taste, you'll love it.'

The demon was still suspicious. 'What's your name?'

'Belfart,' Adam said, remembering the name of the goblin in the witch's castle who wanted to join the Marines. The demon snorted.

'That sounds like a goblin's name,' he said. 'Where are you from? I haven't seen you round here before.'

Adam didn't believe he could stand a lengthy questioning. He decided to act more annoyed, more like a real demon.

'Listen,' he said impatiently. 'If you don't want this blood, it's fine with me.' He raised the glass to his lips. 'I'm not that full after all. I think I'll just finish it myself. Hmm – this is going to be good. Nothing like a glass of *warm* human juice in the evening.'

The demon didn't like that. In a swift move, he grabbed the glass from Adam's hand and swallowed the drink in one gulp. Then the glass fell from the demon's hand as he stared at Adam with the most peculiar expression, even for a demon.

'That must have been a cold kid,' he mumbled.

Then the demon's eyes closed and he fainted on the sand.

'Hurry!' Adam called to the others, who watched from behind the jetty.

It was almost dark by the time they were able to drag Bryce's demon to the cemetery. The demon weighed more than they would have thought for such a small guy. Watch, Adam and Sally had to do all the work. Bryce continued to maintain it was not safe for him to touch his counterpart. He told them to lay the demon beside the tombstone, but not touching it.

'He will wake up as soon as we put his hand on the portal,' Bryce said.

'You know an awful lot about demons,' Watch remarked.

'You know how everything works here,' Adam nodded.

'That's because I've kept my eyes and ears open since I got here,' Bryce said sternly. 'If you had done the same you wouldn't be in the mess you are now. You wouldn't have rushed off to meet your counterparts.'

'They sometimes make poor decisions,' Sally said quietly.

'Night's coming,' Adam said. 'How are we supposed to survive here until you return with our demons?'

'You will just have to do the best you can,' Bryce said. 'But whatever you do, try to stay round here. I can't say exactly when I'll be shoving your demons through, but you have to be right here. Otherwise you won't get back.'

'What do we do when you shove them through?' Watch asked.

'The portal will open,' Bryce said. 'You just jump through.'

'Do you know where Cindy lives?' Adam asked.

'Yes,' Bryce said. 'I'll go straight to her house and see how she is. I promise.' He nodded to his demon slumped on the ground. 'Now press his palm against the tombstone. Like I said, it will probably wake him up. You must be prepared to fight him off.'

'How do we do that?' Sally asked, suddenly not so sure about her super-hero.

'Do the best you can. I'll return as soon as I can.' Bryce paused and glanced around. 'Place his hand on the tombstone. Do it now.'

Adam did as Bryce said. Several things happened simultaneously. The tombstone glowed with a strange white light and Bryce leapt into it and disappeared, taking his knapsack with him. Then the demon was shaking his head and opening his eyes and looking angrily around.

'Hey,' he said when he saw them. 'You're the humans I heard about. You're the ones with the warm blood. Come here, I'm thirsty.'

# Nine

When the knock came on the door, Cindy almost screamed. Her mother had gone out for the evening, and her little brother had a cold and had already gone to bed early. In a sense she was all alone in the house. But even though it wasn't completely dark, she was terrified to be alone. Ever since she had said goodbye to Adam, Watch and Sally, she had been trembling. They had said that they would be coming back for her. They were her friends, but just the thought of seeing them again terrified her.

And she did not know why.

She was so confused.

Her brain felt as if it was working underwater.

The person knocked again at the front door.

Cindy felt like crying. She wanted to remain silent and hope they went away. She tried that, in fact, but whoever was at the door was persistent. The knocking continued, growing harder and harder. Clutching a folded magazine for protection, foolishly, she crept to the door.

'Who is it?' she called softly through the door.

There was a pause. 'This is Bryce Poole. Are you Cindy?'

She coughed. 'What do you want?'

'I have to talk to you. It's important. Open the door.'

'No. I don't know you. Go away. Come back tomorrow.'

'I can't. This is an emergency. Your friends are in danger.'

'My friends,' Cindy muttered, not sure how she was supposed to complete the sentence. She didn't want to talk about her friends, she didn't want to see them. Yet they had told her they were coming back for her. Why did that thought fill her with dread? She saw them practically every day.

'Open the door,' Bryce demanded.

'What do you want?' Cindy asked again. 'My friends are not here.'

Again Bryce paused. 'I know,' he said quietly, so softly she almost didn't hear him through the door. 'They're trapped on the other side of the Secret Path.'

Cindy choked. 'That's impossible. I saw them.'

'It wasn't them, Cindy. It was demons who had stolen their form. Please open the door.'

Cindy finally did as she was told. Bryce practically jumped inside, and then quickly closed the door behind him. Cindy was pleased to see he was as handsome as Sally had said. Unfortunately she was not in the mood to enjoy his company. He stared at her anxiously.

'What?' she muttered.

'Look into my eyes,' he ordered.

'Why?'

'Do it!'

Cindy stared into his eyes, and as she did so the memory of staring into other eyes, much darker eyes, came back to her. Sally, Watch, Adam – they had done something to her with their stares! Cruel red flames blazed in her head, even though she felt a terrible chill in the pit of her stomach. She turned away and buried her face in her hands, tears burning her eyes.

'What is happening to me?' she said.

Bryce put a hand on her shoulder. 'The demons used their power on you. They tried to bend your will to theirs. But it's all right now. The spell is broken.'

She looked at him. 'Who are you? How do you know about demons?'

'Sally told you about me. My name is Bryce Poole. For a long time I have been exploring the many sides of the Secret Path. There I discovered many wonderful things, and many horrible things. I have just come from the worst place of them all – the Dark Corner. Your friends are trapped there now. They cannot return to this dimension until we capture their counterpart demons and force them back through the inter-dimensional portal.'

Cindy put a hand to her head. She couldn't keep up. 'I don't understand. My friends returned through the Secret Path. I saw them. I went and ate with them.'

Bryce shook his head. 'Those were not human beings who returned. They were demons. You must have noticed how strangely they acted. Even when a demon tries to hide it, his cruelty still comes out. And I know they used their eyes on you. That's why you feel so confused. But the worst of it has passed. You're free to do what you wish. You can help me if you want, and I need your help.'

Cindy had to take a breath. 'They were acting so oddly. I do remember staring into their eyes and seeing fire. But then, everything after that is mixed-up.' She paused. 'This is like some kind of nightmare. I just want to wake up.'

Bryce was grim. 'There will be no relief until we get your friends back. Tell me, what time did the demons say they would come back for you?'

Cindy strained to remember. 'I don't know. They didn't give a time. But I got the impression it would be late at night. I know there were things they wanted to do first.'

'What kind of things?'

'I don't know! If they're demons, like you say, could they hurt other people?'

A shadow crossed Bryce's face. 'They can do much worse than hurt people. They can drag them back to the Dark Corner, to the Gatekeepers.'

'Who are they?' Cindy gasped.

Bryce shook his head. 'It's better not to talk about them, not when it's almost dark.' He stepped to the window and peered out through a crack in the drawn curtains. For the first time Cindy noticed he carried a knapsack. 'We must search for them, stop them before they capture any more people.'

'Shouldn't we get help?' Cindy asked.

'No one will help us. No one will believe us. We have to do this ourselves, and we must do it now.'

'But I can't leave. I'm watching my little brother. He's asleep upstairs.'

'It's better you do leave him here. It will be safer for him. Remember, the demons want you in particular. Your brother will keep sleeping. He won't know anything is wrong.'

'But where will we look for them? They could be anywhere.'

Bryce was thoughtful. 'Each of these demons is the counterpart of one of your friends. Even though they are completely evil, they are connected to Adam, Watch and Sally. There is a good chance that they would do what those guys would do after returning through the Secret Path.'

'You mean, go home?' Cindy asked, horrified at the thought.

Bryce nodded. 'It's possible. At least it gives us a place to try to pick up their trail. Let's hurry to Adam's house. It's closest to here and Adam is the natural leader of the group. His demon probably is as well.'

'What do we do when we catch up with them?'

Bryce allowed a faint smile. 'I have studied these monsters for a long time. Don't worry, I have a few tricks up my sleeve.'

# *Ten*

Adam was never so doubtful of Bryce as when Bryce's demon woke up and tried to attack them. Adam felt as if Bryce had set the whole situation up. Of course Adam didn't have much of a chance to be angry at Bryce. Not with the demon climbing to his feet and demanding their blood. The demon eyed Adam up and down. Adam still had his demon costume on, except for the head, which sort of ruined the effect.

'Hey,' the demon said. 'You're the one who gave me that red coloured ice-cold lemonade. That gave me a terrible headache. You owe me. Give me your arm and open your veins.'

'You think he would at least say please after making a request like that,' Sally remarked.

'Grab some sticks!' Adam yelled, reaching for a branch himself. The trouble was, in this particular dimension, there weren't a lot of stiff branches lying about. Adam came up with a stick that probably wouldn't have frightened a goblin, never mind a demon. The others fared about as well. Yet the demon seemed dismayed at their arming themselves. He continued to rub his ugly head.

'I am not in the mood to fight,' he said. 'But if you wish to surrender, I will be happy to drink your blood and bring your cursed souls before the Gatekeepers.'

'Somehow that doesn't appeal to us,' Sally said.

The demon turned away. 'Then I'm going for my partners. They'll be more than happy to fight with you, and eat you alive. Stay here until we get back.'

Adam shook his head as the demon left. 'Bryce gave us the same instruction. And it looks like it's going to get us killed, or worse.'

'You have to quit blaming Bryce for all our problems,' Sally said.

'We could blame you,' Watch said.

Adam sighed and threw down his feeble stick. 'I don't want to blame anyone. I just want to get home. But it doesn't look like we'll be able to stay here long. But if we leave we'll miss our chance to get back through the portal.'

'That is if Bryce returns with our demons,' Watch

said. 'For all we know he could be at home already, watching TV.'

'Maybe a *Twilight Zone* rerun,' Adam agreed. 'To remember us by.'

'I have faith in Bryce,' Sally said. 'If he can't save us, at least he'll die trying.'

'That should be the least he does after leaving us here,' Watch grumbled. He checked his watches. 'They've stopped. This dimension's got heavy time distortion on top of everything else.'

'We've got to come up with a plan of action,' Adam said. 'Sorehead and his friends will be back soon.' He paused. 'The only thing I can think of is to run.'

'Can demons run fast?' Sally asked.

'We're not exactly experts on demons,' Watch said. Sally frowned. 'You're in a bad mood.'

'It must be because I'm about to be tortured to death,' Watch said. He turned to Adam. 'Where should we run to?'

'I've been thinking about that,' Adam said. 'This place is gross and disgusting but it mirrors our Spooksville in its layout. I was thinking it probably has a chapel in the same place our town has a chapel. We might be able to hide there for a while. I imagine demons would want to stay away from there.'

'But we have to time our return to this spot to match Bryce's return with our demons,' Watch said. 'And that is next to impossible with the time differences and Sorehead and his friends chasing after us.'

'We will just have to hope for the best,' Adam said, cocking his head to the side. 'Do you guys hear that?'

Sally jumped. 'Yeah. It sounds like a bunch of screaming demons, coming this way. That Sorehead sure moves fast.'

Adam began to back up. 'We'd better do the same. Let's head out the back way, and circle round to the chapel. I just hope we can make it that far.'

'I just hope the demons don't hold parties there,' Sally muttered.

Somehow they managed to make it to the chapel, but the going was rough. It was fully night now and the dark had brought about more evil changes in the town. In many places huge fissures had opened in the ground, out of which shone steaming red light. Adam, Sally and Watch thought they heard pitiful screams from these holes as they ran by.

Yet the chapel looked much as it did in normal Spooksville, perhaps a bit the worse for neglect. The place definitely needed painting and a good cleaning, but the walls and windows were reasonably intact. In fact the chapel was one of the best-kept buildings in the entire Dark Corner, and Adam felt a measure of relief. He was sure the demons could not enter the building. Hurrying inside, he locked the door behind them and hoped they would be safe for the time being.

'Maybe we should go to church more often,' Watch said, looking round.

'It would be a safer place to hang out than the cemetery,' Sally said, plopping down in one of the pews.

'But not as exciting,' Adam said, trudging towards the altar.

'I could use a little less excitement in my life,' Watch said.

Sally was astounded. 'I cannot believe you said that. The Fearless Watch, who is always ready for the next big adventure.'

Watch removed his glasses and cleaned them on his shirt. 'I am still disgusted that we will probably be tortured and eaten before dawn.'

Adam spun round near the altar and looked back at his friends. 'I hear the mob again! They're coming this way!'

It was true. The howls were growing louder by the second.

Sally jumped up. 'We have to get out of here!'

Watch put his ear to the back door. 'No. It's too late. They're already on the same street. We'd be cut down as soon as we stepped outside. We've just got to trust that they will not enter this holy building.'

'Is any building holy in this evil dimension?' Sally asked.

The demons surrounded them a minute later. Adam and his friends could see them through the stained glass windows: dozens of them, their burning torches sending shafts of wicked light across the wooden pews. Their hideous faces glaring at them with hunger. Yet in the midst of the attack Adam smiled.

'See,' he said. 'We're safe. They're afraid to come inside.'

But a minute later the gang smelled smoke.

The demons were not afraid to set the chapel on fire.

# *Eleven*

Cindy and Bryce caught up with the demons outside Adam's house. Apparently Adam's family was out for the evening. The front door of the house lay wide open and the stereo blared on to the front lawn. The demons danced on the grass, kicking and spitting on each other as they did so. They had the radio tuned in to a heavy metal station. Cindy peered at them from round the side of the neighbouring house.

'They look like they're having fun,' she said, having doubts about Bryce's story.

'They're just getting warmed up for a night of destruction and evil,' Bryce said.

'Is it possible you're wrong?' Cindy asked. 'Maybe they weren't changed on the other side.'

'You forget,' Bryce said. 'I was with the real Adam, Watch and Sally. These are definitely impostors.' He

71

nodded. 'See how they spit and curse each other. Is that normal?'

'For Sally it's not completely unusual.' Cindy paused and listened as the three characters giggled together. A chill went through her body and once again she saw the cold red flames in her mind. 'Never mind,' she said quickly. 'I believe you. What do you want to do?'

'We have to grab their attention and force them to follow us.' Bryce dug in his knapsack. 'We have to lead them into a place where they're most vulnerable, but a place they'll still be drawn to enter.'

'Where's that?' Cindy asked.

Bryce pulled a couple of flares out of his bag. 'A meat locker at the grocery store. Demons are always hungry for raw meat. When they see it they lose all control. They run towards it and start eating. But if they run into a meat locker, and we're able to shut the door on them and lock them inside, they'll soon pass out. Demons can't stand the cold. In fact, they'll remain unconscious for a while. During that time we should be able to drag them up to the cemetery and open the Secret Path so that we can rescue your friends.'

Cindy thought his plan was brilliant, except for a few small details. 'How do we get them to follow us into a meat locker?'

Bryce gestured with the flares. 'If we light one of these, they'll be drawn to the burning red light. It reminds them of the Dark Corner. They hate the evil realm but it's the only place they really feel comfortable.' He stopped and glanced around. 'But demons are fast on their feet. We should have bikes to keep ahead of them.'

'Adam has a bike in his garage,' Cindy said. 'Wait! He has two of them. Adam's father has more tools than Watch has. For that reason, yesterday Watch left his bike in Adam's garage. He was going to work on it tomorrow, but it's not so broken we couldn't ride it. If we sneak round the side of Adam's house, we should be able to get both bikes. There's a side entrance into the garage.'

'Good,' Bryce said. 'Then he stopped. 'But maybe you should wait here. I can do this myself. There's no reason you should risk your life.'

Cindy smiled darkly. 'My friends are in danger. That's the best reason why I should risk my life. Plus I can probably out-pedal you. None of the others can keep up with me.' She held out her hand. 'Give me one of those flares.'

'Maybe I do need you,' Bryce admitted as he reluctantly handed over one of the flares. 'You realise to get them into the meat locker at the grocery store that one of us has to run into the locker ahead of them. Then the other one will have to close the door on the demons.'

Cindy swallowed. 'And on the person inside?'

'Yes. The demons might kill whoever's inside before the cold slows them down enough to disable them. Promise me, if I get there first, you've got to shut me inside with them. You can't hesitate.'

'Will you shut me inside with them?' Cindy asked.

Bryce spoke gravely. 'I'll have no choice. It will be the only way to stop them.'

Cindy nodded weakly. 'I understand. Let's do it now, before I have too much time to think about it and get scared.'

Sneaking around the side of Adam's house and into his garage was not difficult. With the noise of the blaring stereo, the demons couldn't have heard a battalion of Marines approaching. But now came the tricky part. Bryce insisted they ride straight out the front of the garage, with at least one of the flares burning.

'We've got to pass close by them to make sure they see the burning red colour,' he said. 'It's the only way to drive them wild, and make sure they follow us.'

'What grocery store are we heading for?' Cindy asked.

'Fred's Foods. It's open twenty-four hours a day, and the place is used to unusual visitors. The Witch shops there every Friday evening.'

'You know her? We were in her castle once.'

Bryce nodded. 'I heard about that. You were lucky to get out alive.' He glanced through the garage window at the demons. 'We'll both be lucky to survive tonight. Get on that bike and get ready. I'm going to press the garage door opener. Save your flare for now. Mine should be enough to grab their attention.'

With that Bryce struck his flare. In the dark of the closed garage, the burning colour struck a knot of fear deep into Cindy's heart. How similar the light was in colour to the light that had blazed in the three demons' eyes at Harry's Hamburgers. Briefly, Cindy prayed that Harry was all right. Vaguely she remembered Adam striking him, and the man falling to the floor. Adam must be a demon to have been able to knock out a grown man.

Bryce pushed the garage door opener button.

Cindy positioned herself on Adam's bike, ready to take off.

The garage door creaked upwards.

The demons came into view.

They had stopped their dancing.

They were staring in their direction.

'Go!' Bryce cried as he shoved forward on Watch's bike.

The demons were as quick as Bryce had predicted. Even though Bryce and Cindy were on bikes and had the whole garden between them and the demons – and supposedly the element of surprise – the demons almost grabbed them as they swept by. In fact, one of the demons – it was Sally's – reached out with long nails and managed to scratch Cindy's left arm. Cindy felt a stinging sensation and then the trickle of blood over her skin. She cried out as she pedalled into the centre of the street, pushing the bike harder than she had ever pushed anything in her life. Beside her, Bryce barely kept ahead of Adam and Watch's demons. The flare burned in Bryce's right hand and the demons howled at the sight of it.

'Head for the centre of town!' Bryce called over. 'Stay ahead of me!'

'I'm trying!' Cindy called back.

'Remember what must be done!'

'I remember.' Cindy replied, but quietly, more to herself. Straining to stay a few feet ahead of the demons, she felt more afraid than she could ever remember. And the worst part was still to come. How could she close the door on Bryce and leave him to the demons' mercy?

And what if he had to close the door on her?

Ten minutes later, that looked like it might be what happened.

For some reason, after only ten minutes, Bryce's flare began to go out. It must have been defective. Cindy knew most flares were designed to burn for at least half an hour. Of course there was no time to take the thing back to the store and complain. For all she knew, Bryce had bought it at Fred's Foods. The bottom line was that she now had to strike her own flare. As she did so, the demons immediately focused on chasing her. Fortunately, just before the grocery store there was two hundred metres of downhill, and she was able to put a small distance between her and her pursuers. Bryce called over to her. His flare was all but dead.

'Throw me a flare!' he said.

Cindy glanced over her shoulder. The demons eyes burned as they had that afternoon. She had to fight not to stare into them, to be drawn into their evil depths. Inside, she could feel them willing her to slow down. She wasn't completely free of their spell.

'No!' she called back. 'There's no way you can catch it! You'll burn your hand!'

'I don't mind a little burn! Throw me the flare!'

'No! They'll get away! I'll lead them where I have to!'

Bryce stared over at her for a moment before answering. 'You can't do that, Cindy! This is my plan!'

'I'm a part of your plan!'

'No! You'll be killed!'

Cindy drew in a deep breath and pushed the bike forward as they hit the bottom of the downhill portion of the road. She replied to Bryce but not with a shout. It may have been she was simply talking to herself.

'I won't be killed,' she said.

The wind flew in their faces. The flare blazed in her hand. The demons screeched at their backs. As she neared the grocery store Cindy decided she wouldn't brake normally. Instead she would slide the bike into the front of the door like a baseball runner sliding into home plate. The move, she hoped, would gain her a couple of seconds head start for the meat locker.

But then what?

They would just chase her inside.

Bryce would just lock her inside.

The grocery store was fifty metres away now. Twenty.

Bryce began to brake.

Cindy began to tilt the bike on its side.

Her unusual strategy worked well, at least as far as allowing her to stop on a dime. The only problem was she went down with the bike, and dropped the flare in the process. She barely had time to grab it and climb to her feet before the demons ran into the car park. Bryce was only a few metres behind her, his hand outstretched.

'Give it to me now!' he shouted.

'No way,' Cindy snapped. Turning, she dashed into the store.

It was a weekday evening. The market was relatively empty. Cindy was fortunate she had been in the place before. She knew exactly where the meat section was, and therefore where the meat locker must be located. Racing down the cereal and sugar aisle, she could hear the demons shrieking at her back. They sounded both mad and excited at the same time.

Cindy dashed into the rear of the store.

She couldn't see an assistant. The meat locker stood on her right. A steel door into a wasteland of red meat. Without looking over her shoulder, too scared about what she would find, Cindy grabbed the thick handle and pulled it down and open. Inside was as dark as a cave, as cold as a bottomless well. Holding her burning flare up, Cindy strode forward. Thick slabs of beef hung all round her, like the forgotten victims of some insane war. She hurried to the rear of the freezer, and it was only then that she dared to look behind her.

The three demons stood in the doorway of the freezer.

They grinned and stepped forward.

'Hi,' the one who resembled Adam said. 'We told you to wait at home until we came for you.'

'We told you we don't like to be disobeyed,' the Sally demon said.

'We told you how we would eat you alive,' the Watch demon said.

The three of them giggled and drew closer.

Behind them, through the open door, Cindy glimpsed Bryce. Almost she shouted to him that she had made a mistake. That she did not want to be locked inside with these monsters. Almost she cried out for mercy. But the shout died in her tight throat. Bryce stared at her with sad eyes, and then he slowly shook his head. His right hand was already on the thick metal door. It seemed he closed it slowly. But maybe it was just Cindy's imagination. When the door did finally close, and the dark settled over her heart as well as her eyes, and the demons' eyes began to glow a wicked red colour, Cindy prayed to herself that it was only her imagination. That she would wake from the nightmare soon.

But the demons just kept coming closer.

# Twelve

When the inside of the church transformed into an inferno, Adam and his friends were forced to flee outside. They were all choking on the smoke. Immediately they were taken captive by the horde of demons. It was Sorehead, in fact, who supervised their capture. He seemed pleased with himself now that he had them back. They were bound at the ankles and the wrists with steel cuffs. He said they were now going to be taken before the Gatekeepers and judged. Adam thought that was better than being eaten alive but after listening to Sorehead for a few minutes he had to wonder.

'You'll be brought before a judge,' Sorehead explained as he led them through the horrible night of the Dark Corner. The surrounding demons kept trying to grab them, and Adam and the others were getting

83

tired of fending them off. Sorehead continued. 'There will be a prosecutor and you will be defended by a lawyer. There is also a jury.'

'Which is these is a Gatekeeper?' Adam asked.

'They're all Gatekeepers,' Sorehead said. 'They just change their jobs round. It gives them a little variety. Next week your lawyer might be a judge.'

'You mean, our lawyer is a demon?' Adam asked.

'Sure,' Sorehead said.

'And the jury?' Sally asked.

'Of course, they're all demons,' Sorehead said. 'You're in the Dark Corner, after all. What do you expect?'

'But how can we be judged fairly if everyone's a demon?' Adam asked.

Sorehead chuckled. 'What is this concern about fairness? We're demons. We're not supposed to be fair.' He paused and rubbed his head. 'Whose idea was it to give me the cold red lemonade?'

'It was your counterpart in our world, Bryce Poole,' Watch said.

'Where is he now?' Sorehead demanded.

'He escaped through the portal,' Adam said. 'He used your palm to open it.'

Sorehead appeared momentarily angry, but then he

laughed. 'He escaped and left you guys behind! You got to hand it to him, he's got a lot of me in him.'

'We wouldn't disagree with that,' Watch said, throwing Sally a look. But Sally, for her part, looked too miserable to defend Bryce any further.

After a mile of walking they entered one of the huge red fissures that had appeared in the ground. Travelling through a cinder-filled cave, they eventually came to a huge underground cavern. The space was surrounded at the edge by a volcanic pool. It was the glowing lava that provided the chamber with red light, and also made it uncomfortably hot. Sweat dripped off Adam's forehead, from fear as well as from the high temperature.

In the centre of the chamber was the judge, the prosecutor and the twelve demon jury. They were all resting on seats carved of black volcanic stone. The judge's seat was the tallest of all, and the judge himself was a big fat demon, with brilliant red hair and purple eyes. He was larger than most human adults. He sneered at them as they entered and Adam received the distinct impression he wasn't on their side. Beside him on his table sat a large black book.

Nearby was a massive silver-coloured scale. It was old fashioned in style, basically two balancing metal plates. Beside the far plate stood a tall thin demon. He oversaw a huge bag of thick gold coins. Adam had no idea what the scale was for, but imagined he would find out soon. Sorehead ushered them before the judge and jury, where he smacked them each on the head.

'Bow your heads to the judge and act respectfully,' Sorehead said. 'Remember, you're in a court of law.'

Just before they did bow, they each glanced over at their lawyer. He was short and chubby, and had a big cigar hanging out of the side of his mouth. His eyes were blood red and his hair was like straw that had been dipped in crude oil. He looked like a real sleaze.

'Can't we hire our own lawyer?' Sally muttered as she lowered her head.

'You can't afford one,' Sorehead. 'You should be grateful one has been appointed for you by the court. This guy's name is Foulstew, and he's not bad.'

'We should at least be given a human lawyer,' Watch grumbled, his head also lowered.

Sorehead snorted. 'He wouldn't try too hard to defend you.'

'Why not?' Adam asked, his eyes focused on the floor in front of him.

'Because we would just eat him if he won your case,'

Sorehead explained. 'We would tell him that ahead of time.'

'Silence in my courtroom!' the judge boomed, clearing his throat. 'The prisoners may approach the bench.'

Sorehead kicked each of them and they shuffled forward. They were forced to raise their heads and looked up to see the judge reading from a large piece of burnt paper.

'This trial concerns the case of the fine demons of the Dark Corner versus the wicked and ill-mannered humans of Spooksville, namely: Adam Freeman, Sarah Wilcox and Watch.' The judged paused and raised a dirty eyebrow. 'What happened to your last name, Watch?'

Watch shrugged. 'I use it so seldom, I forgot it.'

The judge turned to the thin demon next to the scale. 'A token against the accused, Scalekeeper!' he snapped.

The Scalekeeper took a golden token out of his bag and placed it on one plate of the scale. Immediately that side sunk down. Watch spoke to Sorehead.

'What does that mean?' he asked.

Sorehead was amused. 'It means you've just thrown away a valuable point. If I were you, I would watch my mouth.'

The judge pounded a gavel, which was really a skull. 'Order in the court! The charges against the accused are as follows: being human. Eating our hot dogs without paying. Escaping from the torture poles. Tricking one of our outstanding citizens with fake blood. And burning down our chapel.' The judge set aside the paper. 'How do the accused plead?'

'We didn't burn down the chapel,' Sally said. 'You burned down the chapel.'

'But you disgusting humans forced us to burn it down,' the prosecutor said, stepping forward. He was perhaps the strangest looking demon of all. He was extremely short and compact. The top of his head was flat, in fact. It looked as if a huge weight had landed on him, and simply crunched him together. His eyes were particularly wicked – they were more like a lizard's than a cat's. Worst of all, he wore a cheap wrinkled three-piece brown suit. The prosecutor continued, 'My name if Bloodbutton and it is my job to see that you each burn for your sins.'

Their own chubby lawyer with the bad smelling cigar stepped forward. 'And my name if Foulstew and I'm here to have a good time!' He laughed. 'And maybe to get you off, if you deserve your freedom, which I doubt.'

'And I'm the judge here and all of you be quiet and

let's get this trial going,' the judge said. 'How do you three plead? Innocent or guilty?'

Adam turned to Foulstew. 'How should we plead?' he asked.

Foulstew rubbed his sleazy oiled hair and took a puff on his cigar. 'If you plead guilty, you will be taken from here immediately and tortured for the rest of your lives.'

'What if we plead innocent?' Sally asked.

'You will be easily proven guilty and tortured for the rest for your lives,' Foulstew said. 'I mean, at the very least, you're obviously human. That's a serious felony in the Dark Corner. It alone carries a penalty of forty years of having your nails slowly pulled out of your hands while your toes are being tickled.'

Adam frowned. 'Isn't there a third way for us to plead?'

'Objection!' Bloodbutton shouted. 'The defendant is trying to take unfair advantage of this court.'

The judge pounded his skull. 'Overruled! You may answer your client's question, Foulstew, but please don't tell him everything.'

Foulstew bowed in the direction of the judge, and then spoke to Adam and his friends. 'It is possible for you to enter a plea of what we call Virtues versus Vices.'

'What does that mean?' Adam asked.

Foulstew nodded to the scale. 'We seat you on one end of that scale, and if you outweigh your vices – when we have finished reviewing your life – then you get to go free. For each vice we find in you, the Scalekeeper adds one of those *heavy* gold coins on to the other side of the scale. Obviously if there are too many gold coins, you will be outweighed and you will lose.'

'But what about our virtues?' Adam asked. 'For each one of those do you take a gold coin off the other side?'

Foulstew glanced at the judge. 'I ask Your Honour's permission to respond?'

The judge frowned. 'Counsel may respond. But let this court warn counsel that the jury would like at least one of these humans for dinner tonight.'

Foulstew glanced uneasily at the jury before answering Adam's question. 'That is correct. For each virtue or noble deed you are able to demonstrate in this court, one gold coin is removed from the other side of the scale. In other words, if you are a good enough person, the charges against you will be dismissed and you will be allowed to go free.'

Adam turned to Sally and Watch. 'We have led pretty good lives, for the most part. We should be able to win this way.'

'I wouldn't be too sure of that,' Sally said.

'Remember what Bryce said. You have to be practically a saint to avoid being condemned.'

'Do we have a choice?' Watch asked. 'I say we go this way.'

'Me too,' Adam said.

Sally shrugged. 'I've been as good as you guys in my days, maybe better. I'll go for it.'

Adam turned to Foulstew. 'We want to enter a plea of Virtues versus Vices.'

Foulstew looked disappointed. 'I would advise against it.'

'Why?' Watch said. 'You just said the other ways we're sure to be found guilty and be tortured for the remainder of our lives.'

'Yes,' Foulstew said, glancing at the jury of twelve demons again. 'But you probably will be found guilty this way anyway. Only this way you might get me in trouble. You wouldn't want to do that, would you?'

'We don't care if you get in trouble or not,' Sally snapped.

'What she means is we won't say anything that implicates you in our crimes,' Adam said quickly, not wishing to lose the goodwill of their lawyer.

'What crimes are those?' Watch grumbled.

'Your first crime is that of being human!' the judge

interrupted. 'Watch! Climb on to the side of the scale closest to you and sit down without moving. And keep your mouth shut.'

Watch did as he was told. Naturally, since there was only one gold coin on the other side, the scale immediately sunk down on Watch's side. That was good. If he could stay heavier than the other side, he would go free. But then the Scalekeeper raised his bag of gold coins and poured so many on the other side that the weight tilted slightly the other way. Watch bobbed up in the air. Adam and Sally were outraged.

'You can't do that!' Adam shouted. 'You haven't proven he has any vices!'

'I just said he was human!' the judge shouted back. 'That is an immediate vice of one's weight in gold. Add to that the coin Watch received for insulting me, and you can see why the scale is already tipped against him.'

Adam turned to Foulstew. 'You didn't tell me that we would have our whole weight against us before we started.'

Foulstew spread his hands. 'You didn't ask, Adam. Honestly, I am doing my best to defend you, and I am one of the best lawyers in all of the Dark Corner.'

'How many humans have you successfully defended before?' Sally asked.

'None,' Foulstew admitted. 'But I keep getting closer with each case.'

The judge pounded his skull on his desktop. 'Order in the court! It is time to weigh Watch's virtues and vices. Bloodbutton, Foulstew – prepare to present your evidence! And may the powers of darkness guide your words!'

Sally sighed and leaned over and whispered in Adam's ear. 'We're never going to get out of here.'

# Thirteen

At first, as the demons closed on her, Cindy just froze. She was terrified. She could see no way out of the situation. She was locked in a dark room with three hungry monsters. She was already dinner. They would probably eat her alive.

But then she remembered the purpose of having tricked the demons into the freezer. Bryce had said the cold would eventually knock them out. Perhaps if she could delay them for a few minutes, she might give the cold long enough to do its job. They were so intent on getting her, she realised that they had not noticed that the door had been closed behind them. Cindy thrust her burning flare out in front of her.

'Stop!' she ordered. 'Or I will burn you!'

The demons giggled. Already their faces were

changing, becoming less human. Adam's demon had sprouted horns and Watch's demon had fangs. Worst of all was Sally's demon, which had snakes writhing on top of her head instead of hair. For some reason, though, at least to Cindy, the snakes did not look totally out of place on Sally's head. It was Sally's demon that first responded to her threat.

'We don't care if you burn us,' she said. 'We're used to burning. Where we come from, we burn every night.'

'Yeah,' Watch demon said. He held out his arm, and Cindy saw that it had begun to grow scales. 'Go ahead, burn my arm. Burn me a fresh tattoo. Have it say that I love human meat.'

'Raw human meat,' Adam's demon added, as he reached out with clawed hands. 'Kicking and screaming as it goes down our throats.'

'Wait!' Cindy shouted. She gestured to the sides of hanging beef. 'What about all this hamburger here? You guys had hamburgers this afternoon. You liked those pretty well. Or why don't you have some prime rib? I'll even cut you a few slices, and maybe cook you up some potatoes and onions.'

The demons looked disgusted. 'We'll eat hamburger during the day if we must,' Sally's demon said. 'But at night we like something a little more juicy.' She came a step closer. 'Like you, for example, you little trouble-maker. I think I'll eat your eyes first, and make you watch me.'

Watch's demon scowled at Sally's demon. 'If you eat her eyes first, how can she watch? She'll be blind.'

'Then I'll eat her ears first!' Sally's demon yelled.

'I get the ears!' Adam's demon shouted. 'They're my favourite piece next to the tongue. I'll eat that first and listen to her scream!'

'If you eat her tongue,' Watch's demon pointed out, 'she won't be able to scream. She won't be able to talk at all, even to tell us how much she is suffering. We should eat her tongue last.'

'I'm going to rip out her liver!' Sally demon said. 'And chew it down with a bottle of beer.' She took another step closer. 'Give me your liver!'

'Wait!' Cindy cried. 'You can't eat my liver. It will make you sick. I had hepatitis as a little girl.'

The three demons stopped in their tracks. 'Where did you get hepatitis?' Adam's demon asked quietly.

'In Mexico,' Cindy said honestly. 'When I was five years old my father took us to Cancun on vacation. You're not supposed to drink the local water but I did anyway and I got really sick. When I returned to the

States and my mother took me to the doctor he said I had hepatitis. I was sick for several weeks, and as yellow as a banana.'

Adam's demon frowned. 'What kind of hepatitis did you catch? Was it type A? Type B? Type C?'

'I don't know,' Cindy said. 'It was one of those types.'

'What difference does it make?' Sally's demon said. 'Let's just eat the rest of her and leave her liver alone.'

'It makes a big difference,' Watch's demon said. 'If she caught types B or C she could still be a carrier of the virus. If we eat her, any part of her, we might get sick.'

Sally's demon snorted. 'That's ridiculous!'

'It also happens to be accurate,' Adam's demon said.

Cindy smiled in relief. 'Yeah, you don't want to get sick. Now that I think about it, I had type B. Yeah, I'm definitely a carrier of the virus. But that's OK. There's plenty of food here. Just have one of these slabs of beef. Really, I don't mind cooking you something to go with it. I'm a great cook. In our household my mother is always working long hours and I have to do most of the cooking. I'm flexible, too, when it comes to personal requests. Any way you want your food, that's fine with me. You can have your food spicy or bland.' She added quietly, 'Just don't eat me.'

The demons looked at each other. 'She could be lying about the hepatitis,' Sally's demon said.

'If we did a blood test we would know for sure,' Watch's demon said.

'We can't do a blood test,' Adam's demon snapped. 'We're in a freezer, not a medical laboratory. Besides we're demons. We don't know how to do blood tests.' The demon suddenly stopped and glanced over his shoulder. 'Wait a second. We *are* in a freezer.'

Watch's demon put a hand out to steady himself. 'And the door's locked. That's bad. The cold's bad.'

Sally's demon swayed and pointed a claw at Cindy. 'She tricked us in here! It's her fault! Let's kill her!'

The three demons nodded in agreement and turned on her.

'No!' Cindy cried, backing into the freezer wall. 'If you eat me you'll get sick! Remember?'

'We can kill you without eating you,' Adam's demon said, now only two metres away. Ignoring her burning flare, he reached out with his gross scaly hand and grabbed her by the hair. Yet he seemed to move in slow motion and Cindy realised the cold was finally getting to them. If she could just delay a minute more, she would probably be all right. Adam's demon added, 'Do you have any final words?'

'Yes,' Cindy said quickly, stalling for time. 'Just before you kill me I want to say that it's been a pleasure meeting demons like you three. I understand you guys come from an unpleasant place and that to judge you by my standards – when I have had every advantage in life – would be completely unfair. Really, considering where you guys started, you've come pretty far. I just wanted to congratulate you.'

Watch's demon seemed impressed, although he continued to sway as he spoke, almost as if he could no longer feel his legs. 'That is awfully gracious of you. You're one of the few humans we've met who understand how difficult it is to grow up as a demon.'

'Yes, it's a hard life,' Adam's demon said, yawning heavily. 'But we try not to complain. Our motto is: "If it hurts, it can always hurt more".'

Sally's demon staggered and bumped into a side of beef, setting the red meat swaying back and forth in the gruesome red light cast by the flare. 'Enough compliments,' she said. 'Open her throat and let her bleed to death. We have to find a way out of here.'

Adam's demon nodded and moved his claw to her

throat. He tried to grip her neck, but his fingers were having trouble working.

'I'm sorry I have to do this, but we are the bad guys,' he said. 'We're supposed to do bad things. It's our nature.'

Cindy met his gaze and suddenly she did not feel afraid, although she had begun to shiver violently from the cold. 'You can't hurt me,' she said simply.

'We're not going to hurt you,' Watch's demon said, now hanging on to the wall for support. 'We're going to kill you. There's an important difference.'

'Yeah, when you're dead, you rot,' Sally's demon gasped, staggering about.

'I'm not dying,' Cindy said. 'Not today at least.' And with that she reached up and gave Adam's demon a sharp shove, and the monster toppled backwards and fell.

And he didn't get up. He couldn't.

Watch's and Sally's demons stared in amazement.

'Hey guys,' Adam's demon called from flat on his back. 'Give me a hand. This icy floor is sticking to my head.'

'Give your own self a hand,' Watch's demon snapped as he fell to one knee. 'I'm too cold to help you.'

'We have to get out of here,' Sally's demon moaned. But those were her last words because right then she collapsed where she stood, and lay unconscious. Cindy could see the others were slipping quickly under the spell of the cold. Taking a large step over Adam's demon – who didn't even try to grab her – she stepped to the freezer door and pounded on it.

'Bryce!' she shouted. 'You can open the door now!'

A few seconds later Bryce cracked the door a couple of inches and peered inside. Seeing her alive and well, he broke into a wide grin.

'Are they down?' he asked.

She glanced over her shoulder. Watch was now lying face down, and the three of them had stopped moving completely. 'Yeah,' she said. 'They're out for the count.'

Bryce opened the door all the way. 'How did you stop them from eating you?'

'I have a bad liver.'

'What?'

Cindy smiled and patted him on the back. 'It's a long story. Come, we better get these monsters up to the cemetery and get that portal open for our friends.' She paused. 'And they are *your* friends too. It's still your plan that's going to save them.'

Bryce shook his head as he stared at the frozen

demons. 'You get all the credit, Cindy. What you just did was the bravest act I ever saw in my life. I'll have to tell Sally about it.'

'She'll never believe you,' Cindy said.

# Fourteen

Watch was not doing well on the scale. Incredibly, Bloodbutton seemed to have a detailed knowledge of every wrongdoing in Watch's life. Every time the demon brought one up, Watch barely bothered to defend himself. And another gold coin would be put on the other side of the scale against him.

Most of these 'sins' were small. Watch stole a cookie from the cookie jar when he was five. Watch tracked mud on the carpet when he was eight. But the way Bloodbutton related the incidents, one would have thought Watch had murdered children in their sleep.

For his part, Foulstew would prompt Watch to remember a noble deed about the time of the last related sin. However, Foulstew seemed to have no record of the good stuff Watch had done, or if he did he kept it to himself. Watch had to supply that information himself.

Finally they got up to the point where Adam had moved to Spooksville and met Watch. By then Watch was about twenty gold coins in the hole.

'Now isn't it true,' Bloodbutton said as he paced in front of Watch, 'that you talked your friend, Adam – on the very day you met him – into accompanying you on a dangerous journey on to the Secret Path?'

Watch shrugged. 'I thought he wanted to go.'

'You *thought?*' Bloodbutton snapped. 'You risked a young man's life just because you *thought* he wanted to go on such a foolish journey? Did you by chance explain to him that there was an excellent chance that he could die on this journey?'

'Bum told us all it was dangerous,' Watch said.

'Bum told him!' Bloodbutton exclaimed. 'What about you? We're talking about you here. You're the one who risked your friend's life.'

Watch shook his head. 'I don't remember.'

Bloodbutton grinned and gestured to the judge. 'Another three gold coins against the accused!'

The judge pounded with his skull. 'Scalekeeper, add three gold coins against Watch.'

Foulstew stepped forward. He glanced anxiously at

the jury and then at Watch. 'Did you do anything noble on this first journey through the Secret Path?'

Watch considered. 'I can't remember.'

'Watch,' Adam called. 'You saved my life by jumping on the back of the Black Knight in the cemetery.'

'Objection!' Bloodbutton shouted. 'That noble deed must be struck from the books! The defendant did not remember it himself.'

The judge pounded his skull. 'Sustained.'

Watch frowned. 'I saved Sally's life as well by jumping on the Black Knight's back.'

'Did you risk your life to do so?' Foulstew asked.

'I guess,' Watch said. 'The Black Knight almost killed me.'

'Objection!' Bloodbutton cried. 'Same noble deed.'

Foulstew addressed the judge. 'It isn't exactly the same deed, not technically. He was saving another person. Also, he remembered by himself that he saved Sally. No one had to tell him.' He glanced at the angry jury and added quietly, 'I think he should get some credit for it.'

The judge considered. Then he picked up the nearby big black book and leafed through the pages. The judge muttered to himself as he slobbered on the pages.

'Let's see here, what is the benefit when one human risks his life to save another human? We haven't had one of these in this court in a long time. Ah, yes, here it is.' The judge's face fell. 'Oh no.'

'What is it?' Bloodbutton asked, worried.

The judge looked miserable. 'By the rules, the defendant must be granted a credit of ten gold coins for risking his life to save another human being.'

'Ten?' Bloodbutton protested. 'That's absurd. A human's life is hardly worth a single gold coin.'

The judge glared at the prosecutor. 'Are you questioning my interpretation of the law? This is what the book says.' He spoke to the Scalekeeper. 'Remove ten coins from the balance.'

Adam whispered to Foulstew, who stood nearby. 'Who wrote that book of rules?' he asked.

Foulstew shook his head. 'It sure wasn't a demon.'

'If he gets so much credit for saving a life,' Sally said to Foulstew, 'tell him to list all the times he saved our lives.'

'I don't want to do that,' Foulstew said.

'Is it against the rules?' Adam asked.

'No,' Foulstew said. 'I'm allowed to advise him. But if you guys all get away, the jury might eat me for dinner.'

'Come on,' Sally said. 'This is a chance to win the case of your life. Even if they eat you, you'll be remembered as the greatest demon lawyer the Dark Corner ever saw. Think about that. They'll toast your exploits with blood in every demon bar in town.'

The idea seemed to appeal to Foulstew. He stepped forward, puffed on his cigar and flicked the ash in the direction of the jury. Then he addressed Watch.

'Young man,' he said. 'Jumping on the Black Knight's back was a brave act. But have you ever performed other such brave acts?'

'You mean, have I ever saved my friends before?' Watch asked.

'Careful what you say,' the judge said to Foulstew. But Foulstew seemed not to hear him.

'Exactly,' Foulstew said, glancing at Bloodbutton and smiling. 'Tell us every time you risked your life for your friends.'

'Objection!' Bloodbutton shouted.

'Shut up!' the judge shouted, leaning his bulk forward as if to hear better. 'It's too late for that. The defendant may speak.'

That was the end of that. Watch was able to list not less than a dozen times he saved his friends: with the aliens, the Cold People, the witch, the Howling Ghost, in the Haunted Cave. The list went on and on. The Scalekeeper was forced to keep removing the gold coins, and no matter how quickly Bloodbutton tried to add a few small misdeeds, the scale kept tilting Watch's way. Soon he was sitting all the way down on his side and Bloodbutton had thrown up his arms in despair.

'Bring up the next defendant!' Bloodbutton said.

The judge simmered, mainly in Foulstew's direction. 'You are free to go, Watch. But please remain in the court until your friends have been judged.'

'Thank you, Your Honour,' Watch said, climbing off the scale and flashing a rare smile.

'Adam Freeman will now step on to the scale!' the judge shouted, pounding his desk with his skull.

Adam followed a similar strategy, as did Bloodbutton at first. Going through Adam's life while Adam still live in Kansas City, Bloodbutton was able to make a significant case against Adam. Of course Adam had never saved anyone's life in his old home town for the simple reason that none of his friends had done such outrageous things that they needed to be saved. But once they got up to Adam's moving to Spooksville, Adam was able to list ten times that he saved his pals from death and at the risk of his own life. Once again he got so much credit so quickly the judge

110

was forced to let him go. Smiling, Adam returned to where his two friends waited. He spoke to Sally.

'Just mention all the times you rescued us,' Adam said. 'We'll be out of here in no time.'

But Sally was nervous. 'But I wasn't the hero as many times as you guys.'

'Now she tells us,' Watch said.

'Sarah Wilcox to the scale!' the judge ordered.

Sally started out all right, better than the others in fact. It seemed as a small kid she had seldom misbehaved. But then when they passed her tenth birthday, Sally began to lose points dramatically. It seemed bad-mouthing another person counted for one gold coin each, and Sally had done little else for the last two years.

'Isn't it true you insulted Cindy the day you met her?' Bloodbutton demanded.

Sally stood uneasily. 'She deserved the insults. She was trying to hit on Adam and she had just met him.'

'Two gold tokens against the defendant!' Bloodbutton shouted to the judge. 'She not only committed the crime, she has no remorse about it!'

The judge pounded his skull. 'Make it three tokens, Scalekeeper!'

Naturally, Sally gained ground when her heroic

deeds were listed. Saving Cindy in the Haunted Cave from a goblin spear counted for a lot because Sally had almost taken the spear in the side. Yet as the trial began to wind down, Sally was still five tokens down and bobbing up towards the ceiling. Bloodbutton spoke about the incident with the Howling Ghost.

'So you stayed down below while your friends Adam and Cindy went up to fight with the Howling Ghost?' Bloodbutton asked.

'That's true,' Sally admitted. 'But when Adam was thrown through the wall and over the railing of the lighthouse, I was there to save him. In fact, I risked my own life when I reached out to grab him. I could have been pulled over the edge and killed.'

The judge nodded reluctantly to the Scalekeeper. 'Remove ten tokens from the scale.'

'Just a moment Your Honour!' Bloodbutton cried. 'We are not through with the Howling Ghost incident. Isn't it true, Sarah Wilcox, that when everything was over that night and everybody was safe, that you took credit for insights that Watch provided that helped Adam and Cindy defeat the Howling Ghost?'

'How do you know that?' Sally asked.

'It doesn't matter,' Bloodbutton said. 'Did you?'

Sally stammered. 'I don't understand the question.'

'Demon prosecutors don't repeat questions!' Bloodbutton yelled. 'Answer yes or no! Remember, you are under oath. If you lie, we will press your face into a boiling vat of lava this instant.'

Sally paused and looked over at Watch. 'Yes, I took credit for Watch's insight. He was the one who figured out the Howling Ghost was actually related to Cindy.'

The judge pounded his skull. 'Scalekeeper! Leave those ten gold tokens alone. A liar cannot be counted a hero.' He paused and surveyed the courtroom, picking at his nose in the process. 'Sarah Wilcox, we have completed your life review and you are found wanting. Have you anything else to say in your miserable defence?'

Sally looked as if she was about to cry. But suddenly her old toughness surfaced. She straightened herself and spoke to the entire assembly.

'I have been accused of bad-mouthing my friends and my foes,' she said. 'To these accusations I have no defence. So I did mouth off from time to time. So what? I'm a young girl. I have a right to complain. But I will say, just before being sentenced, that you demons are the sorriest looking bunch of monsters I have ever seen. You live in a dump and you smell like garbage.' She raised her voice. 'I take it as a compliment to be found guilty by a bunch of losers like you!'

Naturally, her remarks did not go down well. Bloodbutton howled for ten eternal lives of agony for Sarah Wilcox and the judge nodded his head vigorously. All the while the jury leaned forward, panting as if they couldn't wait to get their teeth into Sally. Watch kept shaking his head and Foulstew looked both relieved and disgusted at the same time. Altogether, the situation looked pretty hopeless. Then Adam shouted over the din.

'You cannot take our friend!' he yelled.

His words quieted the commotion, but the judge was smiling contemptuously. 'Your friend will be found guilty, Adam,' he said. 'Have no doubt about that. You may as well say your goodbyes now.'

The realisation finally hit Sally that she was doomed. 'Goodbye guys. Sorry I wasn't the super-hero that you were. I promise I won't ever criticise you again.'

'Soon you won't have a tongue to criticise anyone with,' Bloodbutton sniggered.

'Don't gloat over your victory,' Foulstew told him. 'It's disgraceful.'

'You cannot take our friend!' Adam repeated loudly. 'We won't let you!'

The judge chuckled and closed his black book. 'You

have no choice in the matter. Just be thankful you and Watch have managed to escape our judgment. You won't be so lucky next time.'

'We don't want to escape,' Adam said. 'We make you a counteroffer. If you release Sally, both of us will stay here in her place.'

Watch cleared his throat. 'Adam. Hmm, don't you want to discuss this?'

Adam ignored him. 'You will have both of us to do with what you want,' he said to judge. 'All we ask is that you return Sally to our world.'

'Adam,' Watch said.

Foulstew suddenly clapped his hands together. He went to shout out something but the judge silenced him with a sharp look. Once more the judge leaned over his wide desk and stared down at Adam and Watch.

'Do you honestly mean this offer?' he asked.

'Yes,' Adam said without hesitation. He bumped Watch and whispered under his breath. 'Say yes.'

'Well,' Watch said.

Foulstew hissed under his breath. 'Say yes!'

'Objection!' Bloodbutton shouted.

'Yes or no, Watch?' the judge asked.

Watch glanced round the courtroom, at the hungry jury, the evil prosecutor, the troubled judge. Finally his eyes came to rest on Sally. She continued to stand with her head bowed, looking more frail than either Watch or Adam had ever seen her before. Watch came to a decision.

'Yes, Your Honour,' he said. 'With my friend, Adam, I offer my life to save her.'

At that the courtroom went insane. Foulstew ran over to Watch and Adam and embraced them.

'There is a rule in our book,' he said, excitedly. 'If two or more people offer to give their life in our court to save the life of another, then all must go free. The rule has never been used before today, but neither the judge nor the jury has the power to overrule it.' Foulstew turned to the judge. 'Isn't that true?'

The judge was studying the fine print of the law in his big black book. 'That's true, I hate to say. Not only that. Those who have offered their lives to save Sarah Wilcox are also permitted to ask a favour of the court.'

'Objection!' Bloodbutton howled.

'Overruled!' the judge said.

'What kind of favour?' Adam asked.

The judge hesitated. 'A legal favour. It is up to you to choose it.'

Adam glanced at Watch and smiled. 'Are you thinking what I'm thinking?'

Watch nodded. 'I hate to leave any prisoners behind.'

Adam addressed the court. 'Our request is simple, but we want it carried out immediately. We want all the prisoners in the Dark Corner released. We want an end of all suffering in this dimension.'

Of course the request raised a stink.

But the court had no choice. Even the demon court.

They had to obey the rules in the book.

# *Epilogue*

Foulstew escorted Adam, Sally and Watch to the interdimensional portal. As if on cue, Bryce and Cindy stuffed three frozen demons through the tombstone, opening the magic doorway so that they could get back to where they belonged. It was then and only then that Watch and Adam finally trusted Bryce. They could hear him and Cindy yelling on the other side to hurry and return. But Foulstew seemed sad to see them go. He handed Adam his business card.

'If you have any other legal problems in the future, be sure to give me a call,' he said.

'We will,' Adam promised, studying the card and then putting it in his back pocket. He was surprised to see the demon had a fax machine.

'Have you ever met your human counterpart?' Watch asked, curious.

'No, but I've heard a lot about him,' Foulstew said. 'He's supposed to have visited here several times. I heard he's mayor of your town, or at least he used to be mayor.'

Sally laughed. 'Bum! I should have known. You two have a lot in common!'

'Tell me,' Adam said to Foulstew. 'That book of rules you have – it really helped us out. Do you know who wrote it?'

But Foulstew just winked as he turned and walked away.

'You'll have to ask Bum that question. He's the only one who knows.'

'Ask that old worthless tramp?' Sally muttered as they got ready to return home. 'Why does he have so much secret knowledge?'

'Careful what you say about him,' Adam said.

Sally stopped and then burst out laughing. 'Yeah, I forgot already! Someone somewhere is keeping the score!'

# *Spooksville*

## THE LITTLE PEOPLE

# One

The gang had never gone on a real picnic before. Not in a meadow in the woods with a proper basket of food, and a blanket to lie on in the sun. It was Cindy Makey who thought it would be a good idea to do it at least once, before school started. And since the gang couldn't think of anything better to do that day, a picnic it was.

Spooksville was surrounded by the ocean on one side, and hills on the other sides. They decided to have their picnic in the hills near the city. There were many beautiful woodland places. Places isolated enough that a person could pretend he or she was out in the middle of nowhere. Places where good and bad things alike could happen, and no one would be any the wiser.

Until it was too late.

'I hope you didn't put mayonnaise on my sandwich,'

1

Watch said as Cindy began to empty the picnic basket on the large yellow blanket they had spread. The meadow was filled with bright yellow daisies. Nearby a stream gurgled and there was not a cloud in the sky. The nearby trees were tall, with heavy branches. Although they now sat in the sun, they had found the hike from the road through the shade rather chilly. The shadows were deep and old in that part of the woods.

'Since when do you care what is between two slices of bread?' Sally Wilcox asked Watch. 'You used to be the most unpicky eater I ever saw. Hey, Cindy, Adam – I remember the time Watch ate half a dozen uncooked eggs.'

Cindy made a face. 'Is that true?' she asked Watch.

'It was for an Easter eggs contest,' Watch explained. 'The eggs were painted different colours.'

Sally smiled. 'So were the egg yolks. Only one egg had a yellow centre. In fact, if I remember correctly, the one egg you didn't eat eventually hatched and gave birth to a small reptilian creature that burrowed in the ground and eventually ate most of the local gophers.' Sally added, 'I think the witch had something to do with those eggs.'

'At least I won first prize in the contest,' Watch said, fiddling with a pocket calculator he had brought on the picnic to work out some calculations for a new telescope he was building. Nowadays Watch often carried a calculator, just as Sally usually carried a Bic lighter. They were odd habits the two had.

'What was the prize?' Adam Freeman asked.

'A twenty dollar gift voucher for the local chemist,' Sally said. 'For the next year he got to buy all the antacids he wanted on credit.'

'The eggs did make me sick,' Watch agreed. He checked the turkey sandwich Cindy had handed him. 'After that, I kind of lost my taste for chicken as well.'

'Is the sandwich OK?' Cindy asked Watch, concerned.

Watch chewed heartily. 'Yeah. I'm not as picky as Sally says. As long as nothing in it bites back, I don't really care.'

Adam gestured to the picnic basket. 'What kind of sandwich did you make me?'

Cindy beamed. 'It's a surprise. You'll love it.'

Sally was amused. 'You'll both be surprised.'

Cindy was annoyed. 'You didn't change the sandwiches, did you?'

'Are you asking me or are you telling?' Sally asked, who already had her plain cheese sandwich safely in her hand.

3

'I don't believe this,' Cindy said as she checked the remaining two sandwiches, the ones for Adam and herself.

'What is it?' Adam asked, already losing his appetite.

'We both have Spam sandwiches,' Cindy said, laying open the slices of bread for Adam to see. 'Spam and sprouts.'

'What's wrong with that?' Watch asked. 'I like Spam.'

'I like sprouts,' Sally said, laughing.

'Yeah,' Cindy said sarcastically. 'They go perfectly together. Thanks a lot, Sally. After I went to all that trouble to make us really good food.'

Sally spoke to Adam. 'Don't believe a word of it. I saw your original sandwich. It looked more like something for building strong bones and teeth than something you'd enjoy eating.'

'If the Spam doesn't have mayonnaise on it,' Watch said, 'I'll eat it.'

Cindy tossed the sandwiches aside. 'They have catsup all over them.'

'And little green things from an old jar at the back of the pantry,' Sally said. 'You didn't look on the bottom, Cindy dear.'

Cindy scowled at her as she reached for the other

4

picnic basket. 'Just for that you don't get any dessert. And I know you didn't fool with my chocolate cake because I didn't take my eyes off it.'

'After you baked it,' Sally said. 'But what about before you baked it?'

'What did you put in it?' Cindy demanded.

Sally laughed. 'Nothing.'

'Except for a few of the little purple things from the rear of the pantry,' Watch added.

Adam swallowed. 'I'm glad I had breakfast.'

'Watch is kidding,' Sally said. 'The cake is fine – as long as Cindy didn't flatten it with all the sugar and *love* she poured into it. I know she was thinking of you, Adam, when she baked it.'

'Better him than a complete stranger who doesn't care whether Cindy chokes to death on the cake or not,' Watch said wisely. 'Are you sure you don't want your Spam?'

'Yeah, I'm sure.' Cindy tentatively opened the picnic basket that held the cake. 'Seriously, I hope you didn't tamper with this cake, Sally. I may be a lousy gourmet cook, but I do know how to bake.'

'It doesn't take much of a cook or a baker to make sandwiches,' Sally said.

'Shut up,' Cindy said to Sally as she removed the

cake from the basket. Adam – feeling a little hungry, his breakfast notwithstanding – leaned forward to get a better look. But he hardly had a chance to see what was left of his lunch when a small green man with a nose as long as a spoon and hands as quick as a fox leapt out of the trees, grabbed the cake, and disappeared back into the woods.

The four of them blinked. They sat in stunned silence.

'Did you guys see what I just saw?' Sally finally asked.

Sure. They had all seen the same thing.

A leprechaun had stolen their chocolate cake.

# Two

Five minutes had passed since the leprechaun had appeared – and disappeared – and they were still in shock. Well, perhaps shock was too strong a word to describe their feelings. After all, they had seen many strange things during their time in Spooksville. But they had never lost a chocolate cake before to an elemental, at least not when they were hungry.

'Are we sure we saw what we think we saw?' Cindy asked. 'Maybe it was just some kid dressed up like a leprechaun.'

'No kid could move that fast,' Watch said.

'Or be that ugly,' Sally added.

'I thought he was kind of cute,' Cindy said.

'You would,' Sally said.

'It doesn't matter whether he was cute or ugly,' Adam interrupted. 'The fact is he was a leprechaun and we have to ask ourselves what leprechauns are doing in Spooksville.'

'We have just about everything else,' Watch said. 'Why shouldn't we have leprechauns?'

'Why would he steal our cake?' Cindy asked.

'Probably because he was hungry,' Sally said.

'I think Cindy means, why does he care about a cake?' Adam said. 'Aren't leprechauns only worried about their pot of gold?'

'That's more of a recent idea about leprechauns,' Watch said. 'Their treasure can be anything: an old shoe; a ring; a hat. The main thing is that it is special to them, and that they guard it with their life.'

'So now we have a leprechaun with a chocolate cake for treasure?' Adam asked.

'It looks like it,' Watch said.

'Since when did you become an expert on leprechauns?' Sally asked.

Watch shrugged. 'It's useful in this town to know a little about every kind of supernatural creature.'

Cindy pouted. 'But I want to eat that cake. I made it to eat.'

Sally laughed. 'How can you be so attached to a piece of cake?'

Adam stood. 'I want to see if we can find this

leprechaun. I want to talk to him.'

Watch also got up. 'Leprechauns are just about impossible to find unless they want to be found. You saw how fast he moved. He could be two miles from here by now.'

But Cindy was adamant they go after him. 'He won't move so fast with a big cake in his hands.'

They entered the woods where the leprechaun had disappeared. There was a path of sorts, but it was heavily overgrown with grass and shrubs. They had not gone far when they were deep in the shadows of the trees. Here the temperature was at least twenty degrees less than it had been in the bright sun of the meadow. They were able to check it on a thermometer attached to one of Watch's watches. In fact, just as they were doing this a leprechaun suddenly appeared in the tree above them, reached down, and grabbed another of his watches.

The creature was gone before they could move.

Watch was upset, which was rare for him. 'He has our cake. He didn't need to steal one of my watches.'

'That wasn't the same leprechaun,' Sally said.

'How do you know?' Adam asked.

'This one was older and had a wart on the end of his nose,' Sally said.

'Then there's at least two of them,' Cindy said. 'There could be dozens of them.'

'Or thousands,' Sally said darkly. 'This could be a prelude to an invasion.'

Adam was concerned. 'Maybe this idea of chasing after them is not such a good one. The forest is thick here. They could come at us from all sides. Maybe we should get back to our bikes and go for help.'

The gang agreed. They headed back in the direction of the meadow. But when they got there they discovered their blanket and picnic baskets were gone. Now it was Sally's turn to be disgusted.

'Those horrible little creatures,' she said. 'That was one of my best blankets.'

'How can you be so attached to a piece of cloth?' Cindy asked.

'Shut up,' Sally snapped.

'Quiet, both of you,' Adam interrupted before the girls could get going. 'We'd better get back to the road as quickly as possible. I think we'll be lucky if our bikes are there.'

Of course, when they reached the road, their bikes were gone. The leprechauns had more than a few treasures now, and the gang had to wonder if the creatures would ever give them back.

'But we have to try to get the bikes back,' Sally said. 'Walking down to town will take us the rest of the day.'

Adam spoke to Watch. 'In all you've read about leprechauns, does it ever describe them as dangerous?' he asked.

Watch scratched his head. 'They can get pretty mean if you steal their treasure. But they're usually so small, and don't have much magic – a human can usually handle one.'

'But what about a dozen?' Cindy asked, worried.

'If you're scared you can stay here and guard the ground,' Sally suggested.

Cindy scowled at her but didn't say anything. Adam paced on the spot where their bikes had been. 'If we go back into the woods,' he said, 'we might lose more stuff.'

'What else have we got to lose?' Sally asked.

'They might take another one of my watches,' Watch said.

'Or our clothes,' Cindy said.

Sally shook her head. 'They're not getting our clothes off.'

'We don't know what they're capable of doing,' Adam warned. 'There's got to be some risk. But if we walk back to town now, we know we'll be safe.'

'But for how long?' Sally said. 'What if they're working their way into town. I say we confront them now, show them how tough we are.'

After another five minutes of talk it was decided that none of them wanted to hike all the way back to town without at least trying to get their bikes back. They figured the leprechauns would not be able to move around so fast with the bikes, not in the thick woods. Of course, they had no idea how long their bikes had been gone. They might have been the first items stolen.

They hiked back to the meadow, and then walked in the direction the original leprechaun had disappeared. Soon they were deep in the trees again, hardly able to find a path as they wound through the hanging branches and overgrown bushes. Dried twigs scratched at their faces, and although it was cool in the shade, they began to sweat.

'I wish the creatures had at least left the lemonade,' Sally grumbled.

'They're scavengers, that's for sure,' Adam said.

Half an hour later, when they were so far from the meadow they were pretty sure they were lost, they came to a cave. It was not a normal cave, though. Sticking out of the side of a low rocky hill, the opening was lined with chiselled stones. There was no question about it – the place had been built.

'Do leprechauns dig into the earth?' Adam asked Watch.

Watch studied the carved stones. 'Not in any of the mythology books I've read. But I'm pretty sure the leprechauns didn't have anything to do with these stones. These are big rocks – the leprechauns wouldn't have been able to lift them.'

'What are you saying?' Sally asked. 'Who do you think is in this cave?'

'I don't know,' Watch said. 'But these stones are freshly carved. This cave hasn't been here long.'

'We're getting nowhere wandering around in the trees,' Adam said. 'I say we go inside and have a look.'

'But we have no flashlights,' Sally said.

'You can stay here if you're scared,' Cindy said.

Watch peered into the cave. 'I see a faint yellow light. There might be torches of some kind in there.'

It was finally decided; they entered the cave. It did not take them long before they found several of the torches. But they were actually more like lamps, carved from stone and fixed in the centre with some kind of dark candles. They were arranged neatly along the sides of the cave, every twenty metres, and gave enough light

13

to walk by. Watch mentioned that ordinarily leprechauns didn't like fire.

'Then we're dealing with another kind of creature,' Adam said.

'It looks that way,' Watch agreed.

'I love Spooksville,' Sally said sarcastically. 'Just when you thought it was safe to go back in the woods . . .'

The cave continued on in a relatively straight line for about a quarter of a mile, until it abruptly opened up into a vast cavern. Here there were many burning lamps, running water and the sound of hard stone being moulded by sharp tools. For the cavern was far from empty.

The place was filled with dwarves.

# Three

They looked like typical dwarves – they were short and stout, with thick beards and grim faces. Each carried a number of tools: heavy hammers, sharp axes, stone saws. They all stopped working as the gang stumbled into the cavern. The dwarves' eyes were dark and deep-set, and they stared at Adam and his friends with something akin to surprise and concern. Yet the dwarves did not appear hostile.

Adam cleared his throat. 'Hello,' he said. 'We didn't mean to interrupt your work. We're looking for a few leprechauns who stole our bikes and our picnic baskets. They wouldn't happen to have gone by this way, would they?'

The dwarves glanced at each other, then back at Adam and his pals. Clearly the little guys didn't understand English. Adam leaned over and spoke in Watch's ear.

'What language do dwarves speak?' he asked.

Watch shrugged. 'They probably have their own language.'

'I think they're kind of cute,' Cindy gushed.

'Wait till they cut off one of your legs with an axe,' Sally muttered.

'If they wanted to hurt us, they would have grabbed us by now,' Adam said. He turned his attention back to the dwarves, who continued to stare at them with their tools in hand. Adam had on a green shirt, so he pointed to it and made a scurrying motion with his hands, trying to describe how the leprechauns moved. He wasn't sure if he conveyed what he meant but one of the older dwarves pointed further down the cave. Adam paused. 'The leprechauns went that way?' he asked.

The old dwarf nodded.

'He doesn't know what you're saying,' Sally muttered.

'He might,' Adam said hopefully. 'We probably should keep going up the cave. It couldn't hurt.'

'That's what we said about the Haunted Cave,' Sally warned.

Since the dwarves didn't have much to say, they did continue up the cave. But now the passageway began to curve and then fork in several places. Once again they were beginning to worry they were lost when the cave suddenly ended and they were back in the forest. But they were not at the same place where they had entered the cave.

The forest had changed.

Now it was filled with more than trees.

There was a palace, but not a palace in the usual sense of the word. This place was made of grass and sticks, of bark and leaves. Yet it was so big, so elaborate, that it resembled a castle more than a hut. The whole structure stirred as the wind swept through the trees. The palace did not look as if it had been there long, nor did it look as if it would last. There was not a soul in sight.

'Could the dwarves have built this?' Cindy asked.

'Dwarves work with stones and metal and jewels,' Watch said. 'They like to be underground. They would never have made a place like this.'

'What about the leprechauns?' Sally asked.

Watch shook his head. 'Leprechauns stay out of the way where no one can find them. They wouldn't want such a big place.'

'But it's empty,' Cindy said.

'It might just appear empty,' Adam warned. 'I don't

17

see anyone but I feel like we're being watched.'

Sally nodded. 'So do I. I think we should get out of here.'

'And go where?' Cindy asked.

'Let Watch and me explore this place,' Adam suggested. 'You girls stay here.'

'No way,' Sally said. 'We go where you guys go. Right, Cindy?'

Cindy nodded, without enthusiasm.

They crept into the palace, and emerged in a central courtyard area. It was as wide across as a football field, rimmed with tied branches and vines, decorated with many coloured flowers. There was a fountain in the middle. It appeared natural; the water splashed out of a stacked block of smooth stones, and then collected in a sunny pool. The gang sat beside it and had a deep drink. They were all so thirsty.

Then everything changed.

First the sky overhead dimmed and took on a green hue. Then they heard a faint whistle echoing in the rooms of the palace, coming at them from several sides. It was definitely not caused by the wind. There was a rhythm to it, and it seemed to shift as they tried to pinpoint its source. Then it was as if the very air itself began to change, to fill with faintly visible figures that

18

seemed to be made out of a combination of sunlight and mist. Yet it was impossible to focus on the figures, even to be sure they were there.

'What is happening?' Cindy asked, nervous.

'They look like ghosts,' Sally said darkly.

'They're not ghosts,' Watch said quickly. 'Ghosts don't build green palaces in the middle of the forest.'

'Did you notice that we didn't see a thing until we drank the water?' Adam said.

'Do you think it was poisoned?' Sally asked, glancing at the fountain.

'It could have had something in it besides poison,' Watch said. 'Wait a second. Something's happening.'

The ghostly figures vanished, as the sky overhead darkened further, taking on a purple colour now. The whistling also stopped, and an eerie silence filled the courtyard. They stood anxiously, waiting for something dreadful to happen.

They did not have long to wait.

A figure appeared at the doorway of the courtyard. It wore a dark robe, which hung over its head and cast a shadow across its face. The figure was tall, thin, and in its right hand it carried a glowing green crystal.

'Oh no,' Sally moaned.

It walked towards them.

# Four

The gang waited for the figure. There seemed no point in running, as there was nowhere to run to. It moved stiffly, as if there were only bones under that dark robe. Yet as it stopped in front of them and threw back its hood, they found themselves staring up at a beautiful woman. Her hair was blonde, tinged with red, and her eyes were so green they seemed to sparkle with the light of the crystal she held. For a long time she stared down at them, her expression serious but not frightening. She did not smile, or welcome them in any other way. And when she finally did speak, her voice was more like a whisper, not unlike the sound the wind makes as it rustles through the trees.

'Why have you entered our home?' she asked.

'We're sorry,' Adam said quickly. 'We were just looking for the leprechauns who stole our bikes.'

'There are no leprechauns here,' the woman said.

'That's fine,' Sally replied, trying to edge for the doorway. 'We'll just be on our way.' She grabbed Adam's shirt sleeve. 'Come on, let's go.'

'Wait,' the woman said. 'You drank our water.'

'Just a little,' Adam said, following Sally and the others as they slowly made their way around the woman. 'We were thirsty. We're sorry if that's a problem.'

'Humans should not drink fairy water,' the woman said.

Adam stopped. 'Is that what you are? A fairy?'

'What did you think I was?' the woman asked.

Watch shrugged. 'You look like a woman to us.'

At that the woman's face darkened. 'A fairy never likes to be compared to a human. It annoys us – it's rude, especially to say such a thing in our own house.'

'We're sorry,' Adam said for what felt like the third time. 'We meant no harm. We'll be on our way now and we won't bother you again.'

With his friends, Adam turned to leave. But just then the fairy woman held up the green crystal and its light increased dramatically. Pretty soon all they could see was green light, and they were stumbling over each other trying to get to the exit. Adam even had to shut his eyes – the light was blinding.

Then it stopped. A switch could have been thrown – it was that sudden. For a minute Adam blinked his eyes again and again, trying to get them to work properly. The sky had returned to its familiar blue and the mean fairy woman was gone. Everything appeared perfectly normal. But he should have known better when dealing with a fairy.

It took him another moment to realise his friends were gone.

Or were they gone?

'Sally?' he called. 'Watch? Cindy?'

'Adam?' Watch called. 'Where are you?'

'I'm right here. Where are you?'

'I'm right here,' Watch said. 'But you and the others must be invisible.'

'I'm not invisible,' Adam heard Sally say. 'You guys are invisible.'

'I think we're all invisible to each other.' Cindy said.

'That's it,' Adam said. 'She must have used some kind of magic on us. Let's go and stand together on the first step of the doorway. At least we should be able to touch each other.'

But Adam was wrong. Even though they stood right next to each other on the step, they couldn't even bump into each other. Adam began to worry they might be invisible for the rest of their lives.

'Maybe if we leave this fairy palace we'll be fine,' Sally suggested. 'Maybe the magic only works in here.'

They tried that, and the situation actually got worse. Because as soon as they stepped outside the palace, they began to have trouble hearing each other. Watch insisted they return inside.

'If we can't even talk to each other,' he said, 'we're bound to get lost.'

They hurried back inside.

'Did she turn us into fairies?' Cindy asked. 'Is that the problem?'

'I don't think so,' Adam said. 'She seemed to think fairies were much better than humans, and I doubt that woman was going to do us any favours by making us into her own kind.'

'I agree,' Watch said. 'This is some kind of spell.'

'So what have you read about fairy spells?' Sally asked.

'That they're a pain in the neck,' Watch said.

'That's helpful,' Cindy muttered.

'There must be some way to counteract the spell,' Adam said. 'I mean, fairies are not supposed to be that powerful.'

Watch agreed. 'There is usually a trick to breaking the spell. It's often something simple, like walking backwards or holding your breath or spinning in circles.'

'Why don't we try all those things?' Cindy asked.

So they did try them all, but they only ended up dizzy and out of breath. They still couldn't see each other, or touch each other. Yet out of the blue Adam caught sight of two slices of somebody's skin. The vision lasted only a second.

'Who was that?' he called.

'Who was what?' Sally asked.

'I saw a piece of somebody,' Adam said.

'Who was it?' Cindy asked.

'I don't know,' Adam said. 'It was just a small part of somebody's face.'

'You should be able to tell my face from the others,' Sally said.

'Maybe the stuff we just did is working,' Cindy said. 'Maybe it just takes time.'

They waited for a few minutes to see if that was the case. But no more pieces of flesh popped out of the air.

'Maybe we should spin some more,' Cindy said finally.

'I don't think that's it,' Adam said. 'Let's examine

25

what each of us was doing at the instant I saw that piece of skin.'

'I was scratching my face,' Cindy said.

'You were probably picking your nose,' Sally muttered.

'That's not true!' Cindy snapped. 'I never do that in public.'

'Now you can,' Sally said.

'Stop arguing,' Adam interrupted. 'This is serious. What were you doing, Sally?'

'Just standing here.'

'You must have been doing something besides that,' Adam said.

'I was breathing,' Sally said. 'And picking my nose. What were you doing?'

Adam paused. 'Nothing. I was just standing too. What were you doing, Watch?'

'I was wiping my glasses,' he said.

Adam jumped. 'That's it!' The glass in the glasses must be the key. I actually saw two small pieces of skin, each as large as the glass lenses. Watch, give me your glasses.'

'Where are you?'

'I'm over here,' Adam said. 'No, wait, that won't work. We can't even touch. But let's think about this.

26

What if when light passes through glass it shows our skin?'

'Then why can't we see Watch's eyes right now?' Sally asked. 'I assume he has his glasses on.'

'I do,' Watch said.

'But Watch always walks around with his head sort of down,' Adam said. 'Watch, take off your glasses and hold them up to the sun. Look up as well, so that your face is right behind them.'

Watch must have done what he was told.

His nose and his upper lip suddenly appeared out of the air.

'It works!' Cindy exclaimed.

The pieces of skin vanished.

'It only works while the sun is shining on those two spots,' Watch said, who had probably put his glasses back on. 'The effect is not permanent.'

'But I think we're on the right track,' Adam said. 'We might need a bigger piece of glass. So that our whole body becomes visible at the same time. Then the effect might remain, and we can see ourselves again.'

'That makes sense,' Watch said.

'It does?' Sally asked.

'We're dealing with fairy magic here,' Adam said. 'The principle is what counts.'

'But we're not going to find a huge piece of glass out here in the forest,' Watch said. 'We might not have to, though. Like you said, Adam, it's the principle that matters. Rather than stand in light that has been filtered through glass, what if we stand in light that has been reflected? In that situation, like with the glasses, we have light that has been slightly altered.'

'As we have been slightly altered,' Adam added.

'And where are we going to find a huge mirror out here in the middle of fairy-land?' Sally asked.

'We don't need a mirror to find reflected light,' Watch said. 'The fountain of water collects into a pool of water. Let's stand to the right side of it, on those rocks.'

'I don't want to get near that water,' Sally said. 'It's what started our troubles.'

'Fine,' Cindy said. 'Stay invisible for the rest of your life. Then we won't have to look at you any more.'

But Sally must have ignored her because a moment later – as they climbed on to the rocks beside the pool – the four of them suddenly became visible. Not only that, they were able to touch each other, and none looked any worse for wear.

'But we could disappear the moment we step out of this reflected light,' Sally said.

'No. Once you break a fairy spell,' Watch said, 'it's broken.'

To prove his point, he jumped off the rocks and away from the pool. He remained visible.

'Good,' Adam said. 'Let's get out of here before that woman comes back.'

'Yeah, I didn't like her,' Sally said. 'She was kind of creepy.'

'Like this is the best place in the whole world to insult her,' Cindy said as they hurried towards the entrance to the fairy palace.

# Five

They were afraid to return to the dwarf cave because they had taken so many turns underground that they were worried they would get lost in a dark place. Walking out in the sun, even if it was beneath the trees and in the neighbourhood of a bunch of fairies and leprechauns, seemed a safer move. But they were still lost. They had never been to this part of the woods, and even when they climbed a hill they were unable to catch a glimpse of the city or the ocean.

'Whose idea was this picnic anyway?' Sally grumbled.

'Whose idea was it to confront the leprechauns and show them how tough we are?' Cindy asked.

'It's weird how we've seen so many magical creatures all in a row,' Adam said. 'Usually, when we have an adventure, we only have to deal with one creature at a time. But it's like a doorway has opened to another dimension, and the elementals are moving in.'

'I've been thinking the same thing,' Watch said. 'And I don't think it's a good thing. Look how much trouble we've had already, and we're used to dealing with aliens and monsters and demons. What if normal people run into these creatures?'

'I always think of myself as normal,' Sally said.

'We all have our illusions,' Cindy said.

'But there must be a reason for all these creatures suddenly showing up,' Adam said. 'Maybe if we can figure out what it is, they can all go home and leave us in peace.'

Just then a voice seemed to speak from the sky.

'We can't go home.'

Naturally, the four of them almost jumped out of their skins. The voice was thick with power, clearly not human at all. It did not sound angry, however, only a little sad. Adam cautioned the others to remain silent while he searched the immediate area. Yet no one was visible. Finally he stared up at the sky, and spoke to it.

'Who's there?' he asked.

The voice replied, 'Pan.'

'Oh no,' Watch said.

'Who's Pan?' Sally whispered.

'The king of the elementals,' Watch said. 'Many of the mythologies speak of him. He's supposed to be very powerful.'

'But is he evil?' Cindy asked.

'It depends on your definition of evil,' Watch said.

'I'm not that bad,' the voice said.

'Where are you?' Adam asked. 'Can we see you?'

'Do we want to see you?' Sally muttered.

'Continue the way you're going,' the voice said. 'I am not far. I will talk to you when you arrive.'

Adam and Watch were about to go on. But Sally jumped in front of them. 'Wait a second,' she said. 'This guy sounds like the big boss.'

'That's good.' Watch said. 'He's the perfect one to tell us what's happening.'

'He's the perfect one to turn us into toads,' Sally said. 'I say we run the other way, and not look back.'

Adam shook his head. 'We can't leave this mystery unsolved. Also, we have nowhere to go.' He paused. 'I think I remember reading a little about Pan. He plays the flute, doesn't he? He can't be that bad.'

'He plays Pan pipes,' Watch said. 'Not a flute.'

'The same difference,' Adam continued. 'It's not like he's a demon or troll or something historically bad.'

'I don't like meeting supernatural creatures deep in

33

the woods,' Sally said. 'I just don't think it's right.'

But Sally's arguments fell on deaf ears. It was clear to the others that they had no choice. Finally, they continued along the path, with Sally bringing up the rear. As Pan had said, it was not long before they reached him.

He stood in the centre of a small clearing beside a stone wall and a small brook. He was half goat, half man. The lower part was animal-like – he had four legs, and cloven hoofs. His face was extremely handsome, however. He looked to be a man about forty, with a dark goat-like beard. On top of his head, though, he had two black horns. In his hands he carried his famous Pan pipes. But he did not look in the mood for music. He glanced up as they came into the meadow but then hung his head once more. He appeared to be thinking deeply, or else he was actually depressed.

'Hello,' he said in his magical way. The word seemed to echo all around them, although he had not raised his voice.

'Hi,' Adam said. 'I'm Adam and this is Cindy and Watch and Sally.'

'I know who you are,' he said.

'Really?' Adam said. 'How?'

'I have watched you since you entered this forest. I

34

do not have to be near someone to see them. I know your names and I know how you feel and how you think.'

'Please don't judge me by today,' Sally said quickly. 'I haven't been on my best behaviour.'

'She's usually worse,' Cindy muttered.

'Are we disturbing you?' Adam asked, wondering why Pan continued to hang his head and not look at them.

'No,' he said. 'It doesn't matter.'

'What doesn't matter?' Watch asked.

'Nothing matters,' Pan replied quietly. 'Not any more.'

'Why not?' Adam asked. 'What's happened?'

Pan sighed. 'It's a long story.'

'We like stories,' Sally said brightly. 'In fact, I might be an author when I grow up. Maybe we could take down your story and get it published. You never know, you might even get a movie deal, being a supernatural creature and all.'

But Pan just shook his head. 'This is a sad story. No one will want to read it.'

'You're wrong there,' Sally said. 'Half the adult population in this country suffers from depression. They love sad stories, particularly when they have unexpected endings.'

But Pan was not interested. 'You don't understand. No one understands.'

Adam stepped forward so that he was not more than two metres from Pan. It was only as he got closer that he realised the king of the elementals was really much larger than a normal person, not including the fact that he had four legs in addition to his two arms. Yet not for a moment did Adam feel afraid. Obviously Pan was too absorbed in what was happening in his own life to have the energy to harm four kids.

'We would like to understand,' Adam said. 'Please tell us your story. We're good listeners, and who knows? We might be able to help you.'

Pan sighed again. 'Very well. I can tell you. Sit here on the grass beside me. That way if you get bored, you can just lie down and take a nap.'

'Why do you think we'll get bored?' Cindy asked as she sat down beside Adam.

'Other people's problems are always boring,' Pan said.

'Not to me,' Sally said. 'I thrive on them.'

Pan looked up and smiled faintly. He had a nice smile, even with his goat's beard and his two horns. 'I have watched you the closest since you entered these woods,' he said. 'You always have something smart to say.'

'Better smart than stupid,' Sally replied.

'I'm afraid I've been more of the latter lately,' Pan said.

And taking a deep breath, he started his tale.

# Six

'As you have already guessed all my elementals have moved into your world. We came through an interdimensional portal not far from here. It opens and closes at my command. But what you don't know is that none of us wants to be here. We have come only because we have lost our homes.'

'How?' Adam asked.

Pan hung his head again and spoke softly. 'In my realm there is a powerful wizard named Klandor. He has been bothering me for centuries, but I haven't been able to force him out of my kingdom because he knows many spells, and besides, I don't like to shove people around, even if they are wizards. He has been trying to take over my job ever since I can remember. Even though he is a wizard nobody would ever do what he said unless he threatened to harm them. In my realm,

I was king and that was it. When I gave an order it was always obeyed. That used to drive Klandor crazy with envy.'

'It would bug me too,' Sally remarked.

Pan continued. 'About a month ago I decided to hold a huge feast. It was my birthday and I like to hold feasts anyway, and eat a lot and play my pipes. Every musician loves an audience. I did not exactly invite Klandor but he came anyway and I didn't want to ask him to leave, not in front of all my guests. Like I said, I'm a polite person, and don't lose my temper unless pushed to the limit. Klandor just walked in like he owned the place and sat down and immediately insulted a couple of my dwarves, who have never liked him. But I told the dwarves just to ignore him and maybe he would go away.'

'You aren't as forceful as you're portrayed in the books,' Watch interrupted.

'I can be forceful,' Pan said, raising his head again. 'When it suits me. But most of the stories you're talking about were written a long time ago, when I was younger and more hot-headed. I've definitely mellowed with age, and I consider that a good quality. But let me get back to what happened that night.'

'Please do,' Adam said.

'Towards the end of the party, when we were all stuffed and getting drowsy, Klandor brought out an old gold coin. He knows I love to gamble and he suggested we enjoy a harmless game, where we wagered small things. He even said I could flip the coin in the air and call whatever side I wanted – heads or tails – and that sounded fair to me. I mean, I didn't see how he could cheat me if I was controlling the coin.'

'But he is a wizard,' Adam said. 'It might have been a magical coin.'

Pan shrugged. 'It sounded harmless at first. We were going to wager only small items: a silver plate from my table; a copper ring from his treasury; a silk robe from my closet; a crystal necklace from his study. He had brought his items with him so I didn't have to trust that he would give them to me later. When I won something, he gave it to me right away. And I did the same – I have always paid my debts promptly.'

'What did you win?' Cindy asked.

Pan brightened. 'Lots of things at first. I won most of what he brought. But then my luck turned against me. I would call heads, and it would be tails. I would say tails, and it would be heads. Really, I had an extraordinary run of bad luck. I think I lost twenty bets in a row. In fact, I lost back to him almost everything I had won. After a while my servants were bringing all kinds of goods from my rooms to meet my debts. I emptied my house, and I have a big house.'

'Wait a second,' Watch interrupted. 'You said you were only betting small things?'

Pan looked depressed. 'At first, that was the rule. But then Klandor kept saying he would bet me double or nothing. Do you know what that means? I had to match everything he had already won from me, each time I tossed the coin. That meant one of two things could happen. If I could just win once, I would be even. But every time I lost, I lost a great deal.'

'And with each bet, the stakes went way up,' Adam said.

'Exactly,' Pan said. 'But I kept thinking I have to win at least once, eventually, and then everything will be all right. But I never did. No matter how many times I called tails or heads, the coin always landed the other way.'

'But you didn't bet your kingdom away?' Sally asked. 'That would have been completely stupid.'

Pan looked as miserable as a half goat half man creature could look. 'Well,' he said sadly. 'Yes, I did. I lost it all.'

Adam tried to sound cheerful. 'We all make mistakes.'

'But not all of us make such big mistakes,' Watch added.

'But how can you lose a kingdom with a toss of a coin?' Cindy asked. 'I don't understand.'

'Everyone was watching the game,' Pan explained. 'I couldn't refuse to hand over my kingdom. I had lost it fair and square.' He sighed. 'All my elves, dwarves, gnomes, leprechauns and fairies were ordered out as soon as Klandor took over. I guess he wanted to get back at all the elementals for ignoring him while I was king.'

'Why did you come here?' Watch asked.

Pan shrugged. 'We didn't know where else to go. This seemed as good a place as any.'

'But your elementals can't stay here,' Sally said. 'They'll cause too much trouble. Already your leprechauns stole our bikes and our picnic stuff. And one of your fairies turned us invisible. Even in Spooksville, you can't get away with stuff like that and not suffer repercussions.'

'I can get your bikes back for you,' Pan said quickly.

'I'm missing a watch as well,' Watch said.

'Leprechauns have a thing for watches,' Pan admitted. 'But I will do everything in my power to make sure yours is returned.' He glanced at Cindy. 'But they have probably eaten your chocolate cake by now.'

Cindy smiled. 'That's OK. I lost my appetite when the fairy turned us invisible.'

'Yes, but that was a simple spell to break.' Pan hung his head again. 'Your troubles are easily solved.'

'But there must be some way to win your kingdom back,' Adam said.

Pan shook his head. 'It's gone. I have to learn to accept that.'

'You say you lost your kingdom fair and square,' Adam continued, ignoring his defeatist attitude. 'How do you know Klandor didn't cheat you out of it?'

'How could he cheat?' Pan asked. 'I was the one tossing the coin.'

'But the odds against losing twenty coin tosses in a row is thousands to one,' Watch said. 'He must have cheated. Also, the fact that he brought stuff to wager means that he had planned the game all along.'

Pan was interested. 'Those are good points. I have, of course, thought of them myself. But unless I can prove that Klandor cheated, there would be no way to get my kingdom back. I can't simply accuse him, he will just laugh in my face.' Pan looked away. 'He laughed at me as he ordered me from my house.'

'That's so sad,' Cindy said sympathetically.

'I would never gamble away my entire kingdom,' Sally muttered.

'You'll never have a kingdom,' Cindy told her. 'You'll be lucky if you can afford your own apartment when you get older.'

'You'll probably be a homeless wench,' Sally snapped back. 'You'll be like Bum, always hanging out at the beach and feeding the birds.'

'Whatever happens to me I'll be happy,' Cindy retorted. 'Not like you. You're going to end up in a mental hospital for people who think they're important when they're as insignificant as rocks buried under the ground.'

'They always carry on like this,' Watch explained to Pan. But Pan was too lost in his own problems to take much notice.

'Gambling has always been a weakness with me,' he admitted.

'I am confused by a remark you made,' Adam said to Pan. 'You said, "In fact, I lost back to him *almost* everything I had won." ' Adam paused. 'Did he let you keep anything you had won?'

Pan paused. 'He let me keep his crystal necklace.'

'Why?' Watch asked.

Pan shrugged. 'Maybe he felt sorry for me.'

'Klandor doesn't sound like a "feel sorry for" kind of guy,' Sally remarked.

'Did you wear this necklace while you were making your bets?' Adam asked.

Pan nodded. 'I had it around my neck. I won it near the beginning, when I was winning things.'

Adam and Watch gave each other knowing looks. 'Did Klandor suggest you put it on?' Watch asked.

Pan had to strain to remember. 'Now that you mention it, I think he encouraged me. Yes, I remember now he said how nicely the crystal went with my two horns.' He paused. 'But what does the necklace have to do with losing my kingdom?'

'Did you start to lose after you put on the necklace?' Adam asked.

'Yes,' Pan said reluctantly. 'But I lost before I put it on as well.'

'What Adam means,' Watch said, 'is whether you lost a lot before you put on the necklace? Naturally you would lose some bets with or without the necklace.'

Pan was troubled. 'It's hard to remember everything that happened that night because it was so upsetting. But it does seem that after I put on the necklace, I lost a lot more.'

'Did you win *any* bets after you put it on?' Adam asked.

'I'm not sure,' Pan said. 'But I don't think so.'

'Why can't you be sure?' Sally insisted.

Pan was puzzled. 'It is strange. Usually my memory is very good. For example, I can remember all my human friends from thousands of years ago. When you're immortal, you don't forget things easily.'

'It is possible the necklace itself made you forget.' Watch said.

'It's possible it did much more than that,' Adam said. 'I'm sure Watch is thinking the same thing I am. The necklace might have been designed to change what you thought you were seeing.'

'Is this possible?' Cindy asked.

'We're dealing with an evil wizard here,' Sally told her. 'Those guys can and will do anything.'

'Let me ask another question,' Adam said. 'Could any of your elemental friends see where the coin landed?'

'They were gathered around,' Pan said. 'The party was in the living room of my castle. But they were not that close, and we were letting the coin land in the centre of a deep cushion that sat between us.' He paused. 'Only Klandor and I could actually see if the coin landed tails or heads.'

47

'Did Klandor want it this way?' Watch asked.

Pan hesitated. 'Yes.'

'He arranged it this way before you started betting?' Adam asked.

'Yes. It was his cushion that we used.'

'Do you have this crystal necklace with you?' Adam asked.

'I have it somewhere,' Pan said doubtfully. 'But I don't know exactly where. I tossed it away after I lost my kingdom. I didn't want to wear anything that reminded me of Klandor.'

'Understandable,' Cindy said.

'Why do you want the necklace?' Sally asked Adam.

'I want to try it on,' Adam said. 'I want to see if it makes me see the opposite of what I want to see.'

'I don't understand,' Pan said.

'Every time you tossed the coin,' Adam explained, 'you wanted it to land either heads or tails. Like you said, you called out your choice while the coin was in the air. But what if the crystal necklace made your eyes or your mind work so that not matter what way the coin landed, you saw it opposite to the way you wanted it to be?'

Pan was thoughtful. 'Are you saying I was tricked out of my kingdom?'

'We've been saying that all along,' Sally replied.

'It was more than a trick,' Adam said. 'He used a magical device against you. What we have to do now is find that necklace, and test it on ourselves.'

'I left it in my old kingdom,' Pan said. 'I tossed it away somewhere along the road.'

'Can we get back into your old kingdom?' Watch asked.

Pan nodded. 'There is a portal located not far from here.'

'But it doesn't sound like we'll be able to find this necklace,' Cindy said, 'unless you know exactly where you tossed it.'

Pan scratched his head. 'I have an idea. If we search together, we should be able to find it. And we can always bring a few leprechauns with us. Those guys can find anything.'

'We would rather leave the leprechauns behind if you don't mind,' Sally said.

'We haven't discussed an important point,' Watch said. 'Even if we do find the necklace, even if we do prove that it makes you see things opposite to the way you want them to be – that proof is not necessarily going to win Pan back his kingdom. Klandor can always refuse to give it back.'

Pan nodded grimly. 'Klandor is not the fairest wizard in the world.'

'Let's worry about that when we come to it,' Adam suggested. 'The first thing is to find the necklace and see if our theory is right. Once we prove that, we can make plans to get the kingdom back.'

Pan was touched. 'You would do all this for me? And I have done nothing for you?'

'Well, I am hoping to get my watch back,' Watch said.

Adam stood and brushed off his pants. 'We're used to helping strange creatures. We run into them all the time.'

Sally also stood. 'Yeah, as long as the creature isn't trying to kill us, we help him.'

# Seven

Pan led them to an incredibly tall pine tree that stood by itself in the woods. The pine was surrounded by grass but nothing else, not a bush or even another small tree. The circular meadow was thirty metres wide. It almost looked as if it were regularly attended to. Maybe the leprechauns mowed it every other week – that was Sally's opinion, even though Pan did not confirm it. The king of the elementals gestured to the area as they walked up to the tree.

'Are you familiar with interdimensional portals?' he asked.

'Oh yeah,' Adam said. 'There's one in our town cemetery. We've been to a couple of different dimensions.'

'Neither of which was very pleasant,' Sally added.

'This portal opens only into the realm of the

elementals,' Pan explained. 'It's a beautiful place, or at least it was when I was king. But now that Klandor is in charge it is anyone's guess how things have changed. Anyway, we enter my old kingdom by starting at the edge of the circular meadow and walking backwards around the tree seven times. With each revolution, we move a little closer to the tree. The last cycle around is the shortest. Do you understand?'

Sally waved her hand. 'Piece of cake.' She turned to Cindy. 'I suppose you will have some excuse to stay behind. A sudden attack of the flu, perhaps? Or else do you feel a nose bleed coming on?'

Cindy scowled. 'I feel fine, thank you. I'm looking forward to seeing this other dimension. But if you want to stay behind and keep looking for your *baby blanket*, I won't judge you.'

'Do leprechauns ever fight like this?' Watch asked Pan.

'Only when you steal their treasure,' Pan replied.

Together, with Pan leading, they began to walk backwards around the tree. Despite having four legs and having to use them all in reverse, Pan was a smooth mover. But Adam found it hard to keep his legs working opposite to the way they were designed. Seven revolutions around the tree was a lot. By the time they neared the tree, he was feeling tired and sore. He wasn't even sure which was the seventh turn. For that reason the switch into the other dimension caught him completely by surprise.

They were in the meadow and then they were in deep space.

There were burning stars, shimmering nebula, spinning planets. All these seemed to be turning on some giant invisible axis. In black outline he could see his friends and Pan standing near. It was almost as if they stood, for a moment, at the centre of the universe. Then there was a flash of white light and he found himself falling.

But he did not fall far. Only to the ground, in a new dimension lit by a soft blue light. As Adam rolled onto the soft carpet of grass beneath him, he realised that Pan's realm did not mirror the forest outside Spooksville, as the other dimensions he had entered had mirrored the city directly. Even the Dark Corner, where the demons lived.

Pan's kingdom was much grander in scope. They were still in a meadow, it was true, but the surrounding trees were ten miles taller than ordinary trees. Not far away were thundering waterfalls, and mountain peaks that seemed to reach the sky. Even the flowers in the bushes were more spectacular, large, and radiant with colours squeezed from rainbows. Yet over all this shone a soft blue glow. The light seemed to come out of the matter itself, from the blades of grass, even from the dirt. Pan smiled as he looked around, perhaps it was good to be home. He gestured with a wide sweep of his arm.

'All this used to be mine,' he said.

'Those were expensive betting games,' Sally said, obviously impressed by the splendour of the dimension. She pointed to a distant mountain peak that rose straight up like an arrow aimed at the stars. 'Have you ever climbed to the top of that, Pan?'

'When I was a young man,' he said proudly. 'I am the only person in this entire realm to scale it. It's called the Point. It reaches all the way into outer space.'

'Cool,' Watch said.

Adam was concerned. 'This is a nice place but it's so big. Is your castle far from here? We want to help you defeat the evil wizard but we would also like to be home in time for dinner.'

'I have to cook tonight,' Cindy added.

'It is not far,' Pan reassured them. 'We should be able to walk there in less than two hours. It was along the road between here and there where I threw away the crystal necklace.'

'Then let's hit the road,' Sally said. 'The sooner we get rid of Klandor – and those nasty leprechauns – the happier I'll be.'

'Leprechauns are not so bad once you get to know them,' Pan said as they stepped on to a wide dirt road that led through the trees. 'They're just boisterous.'

'There are many kids in our prisons across our country who would say the same thing,' Sally said.

'There are a few people on death row who would say the same thing,' Watch added.

They were a mile along the road when they were attacked.

Arrows flew out of the trees. One struck Watch in the lower leg before they knew what was happening. Letting out a painful cry, Watch crumpled to his knees and grabbed his calf. Adam jumped to his side and knelt down.

'Can you walk?' Adam shouted.

Watch shook his head, trying to pull the arrow out. Already the blood was staining his trouser leg. 'No. Take cover, save yourselves.'

The arrows continued to fly from the woods.

One struck Sally in her hair, where it got caught, and almost caused her to faint. Cindy hurried to Watch's side and tried to help him up.

'We have to get him off this road!' she cried.

'It hurts too much!' Watch moaned. 'Leave me.'

'We won't leave you,' Pan said, reaching down with a strong arm. 'Help him on to my back before another one of their arrows hits us.'

Adam and Cindy lifted Watch up under his arms and somehow managed to get him on to Pan's back. Without another word the gang dashed into the woods on the opposite side of the road, away from the flying arrows. The trees were so dense, they were able to hide quickly. They helped Watch off Pan's back and set him down on the moist earth. Crouching behind thick bushes, they peered back the way they had come. The arrows had stopped and for the moment the attack seemed to be over. Pan bent down and studied Watch's wound. The arrow was still stuck in Watch's leg but the bleeding was not too bad. Pan shook his head sadly.

'We were attacked by elves,' he said. 'This is an elf arrow.'

'But I thought you said all the elementals followed you into Spooksville's forest?' Adam asked.

Pan was grim. 'Most of them did. But a few didn't want to leave their lands, and were allowed to stay by swearing allegiance to Klandor. The evil wizard probably sent them to guard the road beside the portal just in case I did return.'

'We have to get this arrow out,' Cindy cried, sitting beside Watch and holding his hand. 'It's hurting him.'

'It will hurt worse to pull it out,' Pan warned. 'And then the wound will bleed more.' He studied Watch. 'But it will have to come out soon if it's not to cause any permanent damage. Do you trust me to operate on you, Watch?'

Watch grimaced. 'I trust you more than I trust Sally and Adam.'

'I have no plans to be a doctor when I grow up,' Sally joked, although it was clear she was shaken by the sudden attack, and by the injury to her good friend.

'Even with the arrow out,' Pan said, 'Watch won't be able to walk for some time.'

'Then we have to go back,' Cindy said. 'We tried and it didn't work out. What can we do?'

Pan raised his head and looked in the direction they had been walking. 'I had resigned myself to never reclaiming my kingdom. That is until I met you four. You gave me hope. It is hard to let go of that hope, now that I have finally returned.' But then he sighed and lowered his head. 'But you are not my subjects. I have no right to take you into deeper danger.'

'It does seem that we have to go back,' Adam said.

'I agree,' Sally said. 'We have no idea how many more of those nasty elves are patrolling these woods.'

But Watch suddenly spoke up. 'No. You can't abandon the quest that easily. Pan, take the arrow out and give me something to bandage the wound with. I can rest here until you return.'

Pan was grave. 'The elves who shot at us might find you. They might kill you. Klandor has obviously twisted their minds. You would be helpless lying here.'

'I'll stay with him,' Cindy said. 'I'll guard him.'

Sally was impressed. 'That's very brave of you.' She added, 'Or else it's very stupid.' She reached in her back pocket and took out her Bic lighter and gave it to Cindy. 'Keep this in case we're gone a long time. If it gets dark, and cold, you can always build a fire to stay warm.'

'If Klandor has ordered elves to shoot on sight,' Pan said, 'then the road ahead will be equally dangerous. Perhaps I should go on alone.'

'No,' Adam said, coming to a fresh decision. 'Sally and I will stay with you. You'll need our help with the wizard. Cindy will stay with Watch. Things will work out for the best. They always do.'

Sally looked down at the wound in Watch's leg. 'In

all our adventures,' she said anxiously, 'this is the first time any of us has got seriously hurt. That worries me, it worries me a lot.'

# *Eight*

Pan found the crystal necklace without difficulty. As he had said before, it was lying not far from the road that led to his castle. But getting as far as the necklace was hard, and took a lot more than two hours, because now – with the elves and their arrows about – they were afraid to walk openly on the road. As a result they had to fight their way through the thick trees, and that took a lot of energy, even for Pan. By the time Pan lifted the necklace out of the bushes, they were all sweating and panting.

'It's not that impressive a piece,' Sally said.

Pan brushed off the dirt. 'Klandor had polished it that evening. I took a fancy to it.'

'Let me see it,' Adam said, stretching out his hand.

Pan gave it to him to hold. The strand of the necklace seemed to be simple gold, a thin band that

61

could be found in any jeweller's shop. The crystals themselves were curious. There were three of them: two clear, like quartz crystal, and the other one a deep blue colour, like a very large sapphire. What made them odd was that the clear ones were not set around the blue one. The blue stone was on the bottom, which threw off the colour balance of the piece. Adam wondered if that was part of the reason it distorted one's mind. He was anxious to experiment with it, and stretched the band over his head, causing Sally to jump slightly.

'Are you sure you want to do that?' she asked. 'Maybe the effect is permanent.'

'Are you saying that my mind has been permanently distorted?' Pan asked, not pleased. Sally spoke carefully.

'I didn't know you before you used the crystal necklace,' she said. 'So I can't comment on that. But I do know that Adam has an extremely sensitive mind, that is easily twisted. Why the day he met Cindy Makey, he—'

'If we can't prove our theory,' Adam interrupted. 'Then we may as well go home.'

'But how are you going to tell if the necklace makes you see things opposite to the way you want?' Sally said. 'When Pan used the necklace before he was in the middle of an intense gambling contest. His emotions were involved. His own kingdom was at stake. You can't just get artificially excited about wanting something to be a certain way. I doubt it works that way.'

Adam nodded. 'I've been thinking about that. Yet there is something that I know I *really* want. I'm going to take a peek out on the road. And Pan, don't tell me what I'm supposed to see. We'll just see if I see the opposite of what I really want and what is actually there. Do you understand?'

'No,' Sally said. 'Just hurry up and don't get shot.'

Adam crept towards the open road. Searching up and down, he couldn't see any elves with bows and arrows. But he was still shaded by the trees. He needed to get to the middle of the road to have a really good look around, and to see what was up ahead. Taking a deep breath, he jumped out on to the wide path, the crystal necklace dangling around his neck.

Adam could not see Pan's castle.

There were just trees up ahead, endless trees.

But he did see a bunch of elves.

They leapt out of the woods, bows in their hands.

Adam dashed back into the woods, back to his friends.

When he found them, he shook with fear.

'Did you see them?' he gasped. 'They're coming.'

'Who?' Sally asked.

'The elves. They're coming this way. We have to get out of here.'

Pan peered through the trees. 'I don't see anything.'

Adam continued to tremble. 'Are you sure?'

'I don't see anything either,' Sally said, standing beside Pan.

Adam relaxed. 'The elves weren't part of my planned test, but I was definitely right about this necklace. It makes you see the opposite of what you want to see.'

'How can you be sure?' Sally asked.

'I'll answer that question in a second,' Adam said. 'But first, Pan, tell me how far we are from your castle right now?'

'Less than half a mile,' Pan said.

'And when I stood in the middle of the road, should I have been able to see it?' Adam asked.

'Yes. It's a big castle. You should have seen it plainly.'

Adam smiled. 'But I didn't, and I really wanted to see it. I didn't have to fake that desire. We're all anxious to get there and confront Klandor and get Pan's kingdom back. But all I saw was more trees, as far as I looked. Also, I saw the elves with their bows and arrows, and you guys say the elves are not there.'

'But maybe we're wrong,' Sally said. 'Maybe we just missed them.'

'I don't think so,' Adam said. 'The crystal worked on either my mind or my eyes or both together to make me see something that wasn't there, and to take away something that was there.' He paused and looked up at Pan. 'That night, at your party, you won many of the coin tosses. You just thought you lost everyone because you were afraid to lose each time, and because you were wearing this necklace.'

Pan's face darkened with anger. 'I thank you for your insight, Adam, and I admire your bravery to test that insight. I see now that what you say is true and I have to tell you that the truth has set my blood boiling. All this time I blamed myself for my foolishness. Now I see that even though I was still foolish, I was cheated as well.' His nostrils flared as he glanced in the direction of his castle, still hidden behind the tree branches. 'I am going to race there, with this necklace, and throw it in Klandor's face. I will demand that he return my kingdom to me immediately.'

'No,' Adam said quickly. 'We must come with you. The wizard might trick you again.'

Pan shook his head. 'I cannot wait now that I know the truth. My temper has been stirred, and it has been ages since that happened. Go back to Watch, to Cindy, and care for them. Return to your own world the way you came. I will take care of Klandor.'

'Much as I would like to go home right now,' Sally said, 'I think Adam is right. You might need our help. You have to wait for us.'

'You don't want to go out on the open road anyway,' Adam said. 'There might be evil elves around here.'

But Pan would not be patient. He drew forth his Pan pipes and sucked in a deep breath. As he placed his lips to the pipes, earth-shaking notes pierced the woods. They went on for over a minute and both Adam and Sally had to cover their ears to keep themselves from going deaf. But it was a song, of some kind, primitive and haunting, and it stirred deep feelings inside each of them. When he was finished Pan put aside the pipes and smiled proudly.

'Now all who slink in the woods will know that Pan has returned to reclaim his kingdom,' he said. 'No more will I crawl to my castle through the sheltering trees. I will ride openly, and if you insist on accompanying me, then you must do likewise. You must ride on my back.'

Adam swallowed, stunned by the transformation in Pan. No longer was he the defeated creature hiding in the woods with his head bent low. Now he was like a fabled creature of old, filled with power and determination.

'Can you support both of us?' Adam asked.

In response Pan reached down and lifted the two of them on to his back with one strong swoop of his arm. 'I could carry you to the top of the highest peak,' he said. 'Now hold on tight. From here to the castle we fly with the wind. Nothing will stop us.'

'Except for maybe a couple of arrows in the heart,' Sally muttered as they leapt on to the road and thundered towards the castle, which now stood like a palace of stone, less than a half mile in front of them. Sally added, 'Now the wizard definitely knows we're coming.'

# Nine

When Pan had operated on Watch, he had not only removed the arrow but covered the wound with a large green leaf coated with soothing herbs. Pan said these herbs not only helped with the pain, but also kept infections from forming. The leaf was tied to Watch's leg with a portion of Cindy's shirt sleeve. Cindy had offered the material while Pan was working on Watch. It disturbed her to look at it now, stained as it was with her friend's blood. Watch noted her concern and patted her on the arm.

'Don't worry,' he said as he reclined with his back against a tree. 'It's not as bad as it looks.'

Cindy shook her head. 'You're trying to act brave. I know it must hurt a lot.'

'It does hurt,' Watch admitted. 'But the herbs Pan

put over the cut are working. They have made the torn flesh slightly numb.'

'Pan must know a lot about plants,' Cindy said.

'He's so ancient – he must know a lot about everything. I'm surprised he was so easily fooled by the wizard.'

'I'm not surprised,' she said. 'Gambling brings out the worst in people. It makes them lose all sense. It's a twisted emotion – that desire to get something for nothing.'

'I won't invite you to our next card game,' Watch said.

Cindy smiled. 'I didn't mean to sound so serious. Your card games are always fun.' She paused. 'But you know what always amazes me? You always win.'

'That's because I cheat,' he said. 'The cards are marked. I marked them.'

Cindy was astounded. 'You're lying, you would never cheat anyone. I know you.'

Watch explained. 'I originally marked them because my eyes were so lousy that I couldn't even see what cards the rest of you discarded. In other words, I did it to make the game even. But since the witch improved my eyesight, I don't really need the marking to help my game. But I use them out of habit – so I never lose.' He paused. 'When we get back to Spooksville I promise I'll buy us a fresh set of cards.'

Cindy laughed softly. 'We don't play for money, so it really doesn't matter.' She stopped and looked around. 'I wonder how the others are getting along.'

'I bet they're at the castle already.'

'Do you think they'll defeat the evil wizard?'

Watch shook his head. 'Pan is not going to be able just to storm into the castle and demand his kingdom back. The wizard will have guards, plenty of elementals that have gone over to his side.'

Cindy was worried. 'Do you think they'll all be killed?'

'I think they need a good plan. I just hope Adam comes up with one before they come face to face with Klandor.'

A small voice spoke nearby.

'Hello,' it said.

Cindy leapt to her feet. 'Who's there?'

'Who are you?' the voice asked softly.

Cindy and Watch looked all around. 'Come out and show yourself,' Cindy ordered.

'No,' the voice said. 'You have to tell me who you are first.'

Cindy glanced anxiously at Watch, who simply

shrugged. Cindy continued to scan the surrounding foliage, looking for a sign of their visitor.

'I'm Cindy,' she said finally. 'This is Watch. Who are you?'

'My name is Sarshi.'

'Where are you?' Cindy asked. 'Why can't we see you?'

'Because I don't want you to see me.' Sarshi paused. 'Are you human beings?'

'Yes,' Cindy said. 'What are you?'

'Don't you know?'

'No,' Cindy said.

'Don't you want to guess?'

'Why should we guess?' Watch asked.

'Because if you guess right I might show myself to you.'

'You're an elf,' Cindy said.

'No.'

'You're a leprechaun,' Watch said.

'No. Guess again.'

'You're a fairy,' Cindy said.

Sarshi sounded disappointed. 'How did you guess?'

'We were running out of names for elementals,' Watch said. 'Are you really a fairy?'

'Yes.'

'Oh no,' Cindy moaned. 'I don't know if I can take another spell right now.'

'I won't cast a spell on you,' Sarshi said. 'I don't want to hurt you.'

'Why are you here?' Cindy asked.

'There is a rumour in the woods that Pan has returned. Another fairy told me that he has come with human kids. When I saw you I thought you might be with Pan.'

'We were with him,' Cindy explained. 'But Watch was shot in the leg by an elf, and I stayed behind with him. Pan has gone along with our other friends.'

'Be careful,' Watch warned in a quiet voice. 'This fairy might be on Klandor's side.'

'I do not like Klandor,' Sarshi replied. 'I never do a thing he says. I am on Pan's side.'

'But if you follow Pan,' Cindy said, 'how come you didn't follow him into our world? Why are you still here?'

Sarshi was a long time answering. 'Because these are my trees. This is my home. And I knew that one day Pan would return with an army and throw down Klandor.'

Cindy had to smile. 'He didn't bring much of an army I'm afraid. Our other friends are all he's got with

73

him.' She paused. 'I do believe you are a nice fairy, and I hope you can tell we're nice humans. Would you please show yourself now?'

'OK. But you have to promise not to laugh at me.'

'Why would we laugh?' Cindy asked.

'Because I am a kid fairy,' Sarshi said, and with those words a tiny female figure appeared beside Cindy. She was at most half Cindy's height. Like the fairy they had met outside the dwarves' cave, she wore a long dark coat and had bright green eyes. Only this fairy's hair was black and curly, and her tiny face was more cute than beautiful. On each of her ten fingers shone a glittering ring, each a different colour and design. She stared up at Cindy with a smile so sweet it melted Cindy's heart. 'Hello,' Sarshi said.

Cindy offered her hand. 'Pleased to meet you.'

Sarshi stared at her hand. 'What do you want me to do with your fingers?'

'In our culture,' Cindy explained, 'it is customary to shake hands when you meet someone new.'

'You want to shake my hands?' Sarshi asked, puzzled.

'Just one hand would be enough,' Watch said.

'Will you shake it hard?' Sarshi asked. 'Will it hurt?'

Cindy dropped her hand. 'We don't have to do it if you don't want to.'

But Sarshi sounded disappointed. 'Maybe we could shake later.' She glanced at Watch's injured leg and frowned. 'The elves should not have shot at you, especially if you were with Pan. That was naughty of them.'

'Are there elves still around here?' Cindy asked.

'No,' Sarshi said with a twinkle in her eyes. 'I led them away from here.'

'How did you do that?' Watch asked.

Sarshi was indignant. 'I may be a small fairy but I am a powerful one.' She spoke in an excited confidential tone. 'I confused them with a magical spell. They thought they were chasing a bunch of dwarves, when they were just chasing little old me.'

'We're grateful you got them out of here,' Cindy said.

Sarshi nodded to Watch's leg. 'Does it hurt?'

'Only when I breathe,' Watch said.

'Do you want me to heal you?' Sarshi asked.

'What do you mean?' Cindy asked.

Sarshi was confused. 'You don't understand this simple question?'

'We're surprised at it,' Cindy explained. 'Can you really heal such a serious wound?'

Again Sarshi affected a proud air. 'You think I am just a kid.'

'You just said you were just a kid,' Watch reminded her.

'Yes, that is true,' Sarshi admitted. 'But I am much older than you two are. I know from my mother that human kids are not human kids for long, before they turn into something horrible she called adults.'

Cindy giggled. 'They're not all horrible. How old are you? In human years?'

Sarshi cleared her throat. 'I am one hundred and seventy-six of your years old.'

'No way,' Watch said.

Sarshi looked suitably crushed. 'Well, I am almost twenty of your years old.'

'What does almost mean?' Cindy asked.

'Sarshi lowered her head. 'I'm ten years old.'

'You're almost as old as us,' Cindy said. 'We can be friends. But as your friends, we don't want to take advantage of you. But if you can heal Watch's leg, we would appreciate it. You see we've been sitting in this forest for a long time now and we're getting hungry.'

Sarshi brightened. 'Why didn't you tell me? I know many food making spells. What would you like to eat first?'

'After you fix my leg,' Watch said, 'I'd like a Spam sandwich with sprouts.'

Sarshi frowned. 'I don't know if I know a spell for Spam.'

'A cheese sandwich would do just fine,' Cindy said. Then she added, 'But if you can rustle up a chocolate cake for us, we would be eternally grateful.'

'And a carton of milk,' Watch added. 'Can't eat cake without milk.'

Sarshi nodded to Watch's wound. 'Take off your bandage and let me see what those elves did to you. Pan may be a great king, and an OK doctor, but he is no fairy. I'll have you fixed up in a few minutes and then we can have a feast.'

'Afterwards can we go after our friends?' Cindy asked.

Sarshi was uncertain. 'Klandor is a powerful wizard, stronger than any fairy. If he catches us, he will probably kill us.' But she added, 'I'll go with you to the castle. I'm tired of Klandor running things. I'll help you in any way that I can.'

# Ten

Pan's castle was magnificent. Made mostly of grey stone and wrought iron, it towered over them as they rode up on Pan's back, heading for the massive front entrance. There were guards, of course, grim dwarves and humourless elves. They stood beside the drawbridge that crossed over the moat that separated the castle from the rest of the countryside.

Each of these guards was armed. The dwarves carried swords and hammers, the elves bows and arrows and knives. They stared tensely at Pan as he rode up with Adam and Sally, but Pan's gaze was hard and fierce. Clearly he scared them – none of them thought to draw their weapons, but let Pan pass into the inner courtyard. Sally breathed a sigh of relief.

'I thought we were goners,' she said.

'There's plenty of time for that,' Adam said.

Sally nodded, knowing Pan wasn't even paying attention to them. He had not spoken to them once on the wild ride to the castle. He was so intent on his showdown with the wizard that he wasn't thinking what he was going to do when it came. Adam said as much to Sally, who agreed.

'Klandor will just deny everything,' she said.

'He will probably do worse than that,' Adam said.

'Do you think we'll be killed?'

'I don't think he's going to roll out the red carpet.' Adam paused. 'I wish I could get Pan to slow down and consider what we should do next.'

'Talk to him.'

'I tried.'

'Talk to him again. It's our lives that are at stake.'

Adam gently poked Pan in the back of his long goat neck. 'Pan,' he said carefully. 'Can we have a word with you?'

'Hmm,' Pan muttered, distracted, as they strode through the courtyard. The stone interior was empty, yet along the tall walls there were more guards, dwarves and elves, who had deserted their leader to follow the evil wizard. 'What do you want?'

'It's about Klandor,' Adam said. 'He must know by now that you're on your way.'

Pan was brisk. 'I want him to know. Let the stinking wizard tremble on his staff.'

'But what are you going to do about him?' Adam asked.

'What do you mean?' Pan asked impatiently.

'What he means is that Klandor is not going to welcome you with open arms,' Sally explained. 'Or us for that matter. We need a strategy.'

Pan waved the crystal necklace. 'I have this as proof. He cheated me, plain and simple, out of my own kingdom. He is to return it immediately or else.'

'Or else what?' Adam asked hopefully.

Pan made a mean face. 'Or else he will feel my wrath.'

'That's what we wanted to talk to you about,' Adam said. 'This wrath of yours. It won't do you much good if you have nothing to back it up with.'

Pan snickered. 'I can take Klandor any day, any time.'

'I'm sure you can,' Sally said diplomatically. 'And we wouldn't be worried if this was going to be a one to one contest. But if you haven't noticed, Pan, Klandor controls this castle. He has plenty of elves and dwarves backing him up. I don't know if you can handle all of them at once.'

Pan was not impressed. 'They wouldn't dare hurt us.'

'Actually,' Adam said, 'they already shot one of us. We mustn't underestimate them. You said it yourself, they have sworn allegiance to the wizard. If he tells them to grab us, I think they will.'

Pan nodded grimly.

Yet he remained stubborn.

'I won't give him the chance,' Pan swore.

They were inside the inner portion of the castle for only two seconds when they were surrounded by a dozen dwarves and elves. Each carried a long spear which they pointed at Pan and his friends, with significant effect. Pan could not just push them aside, and so his temper grew worse.

'You're my subjects!' he hollered. 'I am your king! Get out of my way!'

They did clear a way for him, of sorts. But they only gave Pan enough room to move forward; the spears didn't come down. If anything the tips were brought closer. A sharp point brushed Sally's ribs and she squealed.

'Ouch!' she said, and then complained to Adam. 'Why do we let ourselves get roped into these situations? The next time a supernatural creature appears who needs help defeating the forces of darkness, we should just say no, we are too busy. We have better things to do with our time.'

Adam shook his head. 'You know we can't turn down a friend in need.'

'But Pan isn't a friend,' she said in an anxious whisper. 'We only just met him today. Maybe we can explain that to the wizard. Maybe we can tell him that Pan has in reality kidnapped us.'

'You can't say that.'

'Why not?'

'Because it's not true,' Adam said.

'Who cares about the truth? We're talking about our lives here. If we have to lie to save ourselves, we do it.'

Adam was grim. 'I doubt the wizard will believe any of our lies.'

They were ushered into a vast stone room. The design was elaborate: there were numerous statues, exquisite paintings. Adam suspected it was here that Pan had held his fateful celebration. At the end of the long room was a throne, and perhaps Pan had sat upon it most of that night. But now it belonged to the evil wizard, Klandor.

He was tall – as wizards are wont to be – and old

and wrinkled. His skin was very pale and stiff; it looked as if he had never seen the sun, and that if he laughed, even once, his expression would crack into something more awful than it already was. He wore a ragged purple robe; it looked as if the blood of many past enemies had been spilled on it. But it was his eyes that were the real horror – tiny and black, like beads spun at night by spiders who ate their victims alive.

These weird eyes followed them as they were carefully escorted towards the throne. On top of Klandor's old head was a sharply pointed red and black cap. The colours on it moved as Adam stared at it, flowing currents of danger. The cap looked like a storage container of energy designed to fuel evil magic.

Pan was brought within ten metres of the throne before Klandor raised his hand. The spears converged and stopped Pan. Adam noticed then how long the wizard's nails were, how sharp and darkly stained they were, almost as if they had been recently dipped in blood. Klandor leaned forward in his seat and held up a bony finger.

'You were banished from my kingdom,' he said in a scratchy voice that nevertheless carried disturbing authority. It sent a chill deep into Adam's bones. 'Why have you returned?'

Pan held up the crystal necklace. 'You know why I have returned! You lied to me that night I won this necklace. You said it was a mere decoration, something that looked nice with my two horns. What you did not say was that it was a magical device designed to twist the vision of the one who wears it. I did not lose all those bets to you. I won many of them, and sitting across from me, you knew that I won. But you kept me increasing my wager. You forced me to risk everything to regain something that still belonged to me!'

Klandor smiled thinly, and the many wrinkles on his face crowded so tight together that it was as if his skin was covered with strangled webs. He looked more than old then, he looked like something that had been dead for weeks, and only brought back to life with the power of forbidden spells and unthinkable sacrifices. His black eyes shone with a cold light even as his hideous smile widened. Adam had the feeling that he was not impressed by the fact that Pan had just called him a liar and a thief.

'I forced you to do nothing,' Klandor said. 'You were mad that night, so puffed up with your pride and position that you didn't know when to stop. In front of a hundred witnesses you gambled away your kingdom. Everyone saw, everyone knows the truth. Now you enter my home and insult me with your lies. You try to rewrite what was. How should I reward such behaviour, Pan? Perhaps I was too kind to allow you and your miserable followers to leave this land in peace. For it does not seem that you have returned in peace. Yes, I know about the four human warriors you have brought with you to assassinate me. I see you have two of them on your back. Wretched creatures they look to me, and unworthy of being even in your questionable company. Have they anything to say for themselves?'

'Yeah,' Sally spoke up. 'First off I resent being referred to as a wretched creature. Now it is true that from time to time I suffer from bad moods, and on such occasions it could be said that I am wretched. But that is a momentary state of mind and doesn't constitute my true nature. In other words, it is not fair to label me wretched. Especially when the label is being applied by the likes of you, since you are obviously a down on his luck magician who can't get a decent gig at the local bar.' Sally paused and then suddenly jerked to the side. 'Ouch! Adam? Why did you poke me in the side?'

'Because I think I should talk to him instead of you,' he whispered.

'What am I doing wrong?' she asked.

'I thought you were going to try to reason with him?'

'But you told me not to lie!'

'Not all reason is a lie.' Adam reminded her.

'You can't reason with an evil wizard,' Sally whispered back.

'I can at least try.' Adam cleared his throat and spoke to Klandor. 'As you can see, Mr Klandor, we're friends of Pan. We don't deny that, although we just met him this afternoon while we were trying to find our bikes in the forest. But we're not assassins like you said. We didn't come here to kill you. We don't believe in killing, especially when it comes to having ourselves killed. But we do believe Pan has a point when he says he was conned out of his kingdom. Now I tested this necklace and I discovered that it definitely alters how one sees the world. And I know if Pan was wearing it when he gambled his kingdom away to you, then he was playing at an unfair disadvantage. Now what I think you two should do is retire to a nice quiet place and talk about how—'

'Silence!' Klandor shouted, raising his bony hand again. 'You have the nerve to accuse me of being a cheat in front of all my loyal subjects?'

'Well,' Adam said carefully. 'I didn't use the word cheating.'

'But he did imply it,' Sally added. 'Because you did cheat Pan. You cheated him because you're a natural born loser. Just look at the company you keep – all these half-baked dwarves and elves. Why I've seen leprechauns with chocolate cakes for treasure that could take this lousy company.'

'Sally,' Adam said.

'What?'

'Please do not speak again until we are back in Spooksville and there are no sharp spears pointed at us.'

'Like you had a lot of success with him calling him a cheat,' Sally snapped.

'You are going to get us killed.'

'Then at least I will die with my tongue working, which is all that matters.'

Adam sighed. 'Oh brother.'

Pan spoke up, his temper unabated. 'Klandor!' he shouted, waving the necklace again. 'You were always good with words, but let's see how good you are with a sword. Right now, in front of all these traitors you call loyal subjects, I challenge you to one to one combat. If you accept my challenge, and truth is on your side, then you will surely defeat me. But if you refuse to fight then all will know the reason why. Because you are not only a cheat and a liar, but a coward as well!'

Sally looked at Adam. 'He's worse than both of us.'

'Shh,' Adam cautioned.

Klandor chuckled long and wickedly. 'You come here swearing challenges of honour and bravery. You, who have not even a place to hang your horns. You're not a king any more, Pan. You have no right to challenge a true king, like myself. But because I am a king I know the meaning of mercy. You will leave my land once more. Should you try to return, though, should we see your face ever again, then you will be slaughtered and eaten by those who strike you down. Goat meat is always a delicacy in these parts. As to your insolent human friends, they are to remain here with me, where I will do with them what I wish. And as to the crystal necklace you won from me, I let you keep it. Let it be a reminder to you of how far you have fallen.'

Sally looked at Adam again. 'I told you how bad he was.'

Adam sighed. 'I'm afraid you were right.'

# *Eleven*

Cindy, Watch and Sarshi ran into Pan about midway between the castle and the interdimensional portal. Cindy and Watch were concerned to see that Adam and Sally were not with Pan. But when they tried to question Pan about their friends' whereabouts, Pan merely hung his head low and looked depressed. It was then they noticed that he wore a crystal necklace. Both wondered if it was the one that was responsible for all the trouble. But it was difficult to get any information out of Pan.

'At least tell us if they're still alive,' Cindy said, getting exasperated.

Pan finally looked up at that. 'I'm sorry, Cindy. The last time I saw them they were alive. But I don't know what Klandor has done to them by now. The wizard has absolutely no honour. In front of everyone I explained exactly how he had cheated me, and he had the nerve to deny it. Then, when I challenged him to a fair combat, he refused to cross swords with me. He is not only evil, he is unethical.'

'Like all this is a big surprise to us,' Watch said.

Cindy was anxious. 'We have to get back to the castle. We have to rescue Adam and Sally before he does something horrible to them.'

Pan shook his head. 'It's impossible. If I go back there I will be killed and eaten. And you'll never get into the castle without me to lead you.'

'Excuse me,' Cindy said angrily. 'Adam and Sally risked their lives to help you. Now you had better risk your life to save them. We are going back to the castle and you are going with us. That is a fact you'd better accept right now.'

Pan appeared crushed. 'Fine. We can walk there now, but we will be walking to our deaths.' He sighed and looked up at the sky. 'Not that I would mind leaving this world right now.'

Watch nodded to the crystal necklace. 'Is that the piece that we've heard so much about?'

Pan glanced down. 'Yeah. I was just about to throw it away again.'

Watch held out his hand. 'May I see it?'

Pan gave it to him. 'You can keep it. I would rather not have to see it again in this life.'

'Hello Pan,' Sarshi said.

Pan frowned in her direction. 'Who are you?'

'A fairy. A loyal subject. I am here to help save your kingdom.'

'How old are you?' Pan asked.

Sarshi fidgeted. 'Almost ten. But I'm very powerful. Just ask Watch. I healed his leg.'

'She fixed it better than you did,' Watch admitted as he studied the crystal necklace. 'I don't even have a limp. She also fed us.' Watch pointed out the order of the stones to Cindy. 'See how the blue one is set at the bottom.'

'So what?' Cindy said. 'What does it mean?'

Watch shrugged. 'I don't know. But it would look prettier if the clear stones were set on either side of the blue one.'

'But who cares whether it's pretty or not?' Cindy asked. 'All that matters is whether we can use it as a weapon to get back at Klandor and free Adam and Sally.'

Watch spoke to Pan. 'Did Adam certify that this thing makes you see the opposite of what you desire?'

93

'I think so,' Pan mumbled.

'Yes or no?' Cindy demanded.

'Yes,' Pan replied. 'It turns the whole brain upside down.'

Watch considered. 'What if we could convince Klandor to gamble with us? What if when we do so we have Sarshi secretly slip this necklace around the wizard's neck? We might be able to trick him with his own tool.'

'What do we have to offer him that he will want to gamble with us?' Cindy asked.

Watch touched his pants pocket. 'I have a thing or two with me that he might desire.'

'But I told you,' Sarshi said. 'Klandor is more powerful than any fairy. I can weave an invisible net around myself, but his keen eyes will pierce it. He will see me if I try to slip the necklace around his neck, and he will know what we're up to.'

'I have thought about that.' Watch fiddled with the bottom blue stone. 'Still, it may be possible to distract him somehow so that you can do what you need to do. To make him believe he knows what we're up to, and have him be completely wrong.'

'What are you talking about?' Cindy asked.

Watch pulled the blue stone free. 'I think the order

of these crystals is important.' He held the stone up to the light. 'In fact, I think the order makes the whole thing work.'

# Twelve

After Pan left, Klandor turned Adam and Sally into chickens. Well, Adam became a rooster and Sally was changed into a chicken. Klandor simply waved his bony arms and chanted a few nasty magical words and the transformation occurred, right in front of all the elves and dwarves, who cheered the spectacle. Then the wizard ordered that the two be taken outside and put in the wire cage with all the other poultry. It seemed Klandor planned on having chicken for dinner that night.

Adam and Sally huddled in the corner of the cage and tried to look inconspicuous. The other chickens walked around and pecked at the seed spread on the ground. So far Adam and Sally had not invited much attention. Normally Adam wouldn't have looked twice at the seed but now it did look kind of appealing. He hadn't really had lunch. He told Sally as much.

'How can you think of eating at a time like this?' she snapped at him. 'We have to get out of here and get back to the others.'

'If we do get back to the others,' Adam said, 'they might eat us.'

Sally was worried, and Adam had never seen a worried chicken before. The sight would have been comical had the situation been less dire.

'But we can still speak English,' Sally said. 'We can talk to them. They will recognise us that way.'

'We seem to be speaking English to each other,' Adam said. 'But we don't have human vocal cords. I doubt another person would understand us. In fact, I suspect we sound no different than all the other chickens gathered here.'

'That's a depressing thought,' Sally said.

'It's reality.'

Sally was annoyed. 'How can you say being turned into a chicken and a hen is reality? Nothing in this dimension makes any sense. We have to figure out a way out of here, I tell you, and soon.'

'You're not listening to me. Getting out of here is only half our problem. We still have to get Klandor to change us back into human beings. And I don't know how we can do that. The guy is completely unreason-able.'

'Like calling him a cheat was reasoning with him.'

'I didn't say that,' Adam said. 'You said that. And probably if you had kept your mouth shut, we would be with Pan right now, walking back towards the portal.'

'Pan's a loser,' Sally grumbled. 'Klandor says he can go so he just leaves. He hardly says goodbye to us. I swear, the wizard should have changed him into something.'

'He does have half a goat's body already.' Adam remarked.

'So put a penguin's head on him, I don't care. What I mean is, it was his kingdom that we were trying to win back and he's the one that gets set free. It's not fair.'

'When has Spooksville ever been fair?' Adam asked.

Sally fumed, which made her feathers stand up straighter. 'We're a long way from Spooksville right now.'

That point was driven home a moment later when a fat white chicken came up to Adam and started nudging his side. Adam tried to push the chicken away but the creature kept pressing against him, much to his annoyance.

'I think she likes you,' Sally observed.

99

'Don't be ridiculous,' Adam said.

'Why are you embarrassed?' Sally asked. 'You have nice red feathers, cool skinny legs. I find you kind of cute myself.'

'I am not a rooster,' Adam replied. 'Don't treat me like one.'

'You're the one who just said we have to face reality,' Sally said. 'Right now, you sure do look like a rooster,' She added, 'Do you think I'm a good-looking chicken?'

'I wouldn't know a good-looking chicken if one was staring me in the face,' Adam said. The fat chicken finally got on his nerves. Using all his strength, he pushed it away. But the creature just jumped back to his side. 'What's your problem?' Adam asked.

The chicken replied. 'I love you.'

Adam blinked. 'What?'

Sally burst out laughing. 'Oh my! Adam has a girlfriend!'

Adam yelled at her. 'Shut up! Don't let the other chickens hear that. This one is bad enough. Anyway, this chicken doesn't love me. It's just a chicken. It's not even supposed to be able to talk.'

The fat chicken brushed up against Adam again.

'You are such a strong rooster,' she said.

Sally was dying with laughter. She looked on the

verge of shedding all of her feathers simultaneously. 'She'll want to have your eggs next, Adam!' she howled. 'You'd better tell her that you only work for the Easter Bunny!'

Adam fumed. 'This is not funny!'

'This is outrageous!' Sally told him.

The fat chicken continued to pester him.

'How come I haven't seen you around before?' she asked.

'I'm . . . I'm not from these parts,' Adam mumbled.

The fat chicken leaned close. 'Are you happy here?'

Adam averted his head. 'No. I am not happy.'

'Why not?' the chicken asked, standing so close to Adam he could feel her chicken breath on his feathers. But then Adam got an idea.

'I'm not happy because I'm sick,' he said. 'I have a fatal illness.'

The fat chicken drew back a step. 'What's wrong with you?'

Sally had yet to stop laughing.

'I have an allergy,' Adam said.

'But allergies are not fatal,' the chicken said.

'This one is,' Adam said. 'I'm allergic to feathers. Especially white ones. Just being around you is killing me.'

101

The fat chicken looked sad. 'Do you want me to go away?'

'Yes, please,' Adam said. 'Go as far away as possible.'

'But will we meet again?'

'Only time will tell,' Adam said.

Dejected, the fat chicken wandered off. Sally poked Adam in the ribs, or rather, in the white meat part of the breast. She had finally begun to calm down.

'Why didn't you just tell her you were with me?' she asked.

'I don't think chickens respect committed relationships.'

Sally was impressed. 'Is that what we have? Now that Cindy will no longer be interested in you?'

Adam brushed her off, with his feathers. An elf was walking toward the metal cage, and he had a couple of bags in his hand. Adam pointed him out.

'This is our chance to escape,' he said.

Sally shook with fear. 'Don't be ridiculous. That elf is coming for dinner.'

'Can we stay here forever?' Adam asked. 'We have to get out of this cage. Once back in the castle we might have room to manoeuvre.'

'Once we're in the castle they'll eat us,' Sally cried.

'Please, Adam, we can't let him catch us. I'm claustrophobic. I can't be stuffed in a bag. I'm attached to my head. I can't stand the thought of having it separated from my shoulders.'

But Adam had made up his mind. 'I would rather die than be hit on by fat chickens for the rest of my life.' He took a step towards the elf as it began to open the cage. 'Come with me, Sally. It will be all right.'

'I hope they don't fry me,' Sally moaned. 'I can't stand fried chicken.'

# Thirteen

Pan had somehow bluffed his way back into the castle. But this time when he was brought before Klandor in the huge hall – with Watch and Cindy by his side – the wizard appeared more frightening than before, if that was possible. The mood inside the castle was grim. Once upon a time the surrounding dwarves and elves had served Pan. Few of them disliked him. They had gone over to Klandor's side for business reasons. It was nothing personal. The wizard had the power now, that's all that mattered.

No doubt that was the reason Klandor had allowed Pan to go free. The wizard had not wanted to push his loyal subjects too far, and possibly set off an uprising. In fact, the elves and dwarves that had been sent to escort Pan to the interdimensional portal had let him go free a mile from the castle. They had not wanted to rub salt in their ex-master's obvious wounds. But Klandor had set down the law with Pan only a few hours before, in front of everyone, and now Pan had chosen to violate it. Klandor could not let him go again without losing face. For that reason the wizard's first words were scary indeed.

'Do you have any last words, Pan?' he asked.

Pan had regained a measure of strength. 'Yes. My friends want to play a game with you.'

The reply momentarily stunned Klandor, but he recovered quickly. 'What kind of game?' he asked.

'They want to gamble with you,' Pan explained. 'Toss the coin, as we tossed the coin.'

Klandor laughed softly, deadly. 'What do they have to wager that I could possibly want?'

'These,' Watch said, pulling his pocket calculator and Sally's Bic lighter from his pocket. 'This calculator is actually a miniature computer. It can perform every type of mathematical calculation imaginable. It can also store data related to one's own personal calendar. You can write yourself reminder notes. Although its keyboard is tiny, you can even write a love letter or a whole term paper using this instrument.'

Klandor tried to act uninterested, although it was obvious he was intrigued. 'What's the warranty on it?'

'Two years parts and labour,' Watch said.

'What's its power source?' Klandor asked.

'Two triple A batteries.'

The wizard snorted. 'Where am I going to get batteries in this dimension? The calculator will just run down and then be useless to me.'

'That's true,' Watch admitted. 'But it has fresh lithium batteries in it right now. If you use the calculator carefully, it will take ages before the batteries go dead.'

Klandor considered. 'What else have you brought?'

Watch held aloft the lighter, flicked it a couple of times so the flame appeared and disappeared. 'This lighter is brand new,' he said. 'Its fuel reserve is at maximum. But even when it does run out, even in this dimension, you should be able to replenish it with another source of fuel.'

Klandor acted unimpressed. 'I'm a powerful wizard. I can start a fire by snapping my fingers. What do I need a lighter for?'

'Excuse me for putting it this way,' Watch said. 'But you're an old powerful wizard, and you ain't getting younger. I bet starting a fire isn't as easy as it used to be. But with this lighter in your pocket – why you won't even have to remember the spell for fire.'

'Are you questioning my memory, young human?' Klandor snapped.

'Not at all,' Watch said. 'But as the years roll by all of us have a little more trouble remembering the most obvious facts. All I'm saying is that the lighter, and the calculator, make living life that much easier and pleasant.' He paused. 'These are the two items we have brought to wager. Two items, I believe, that are difficult if not impossible to obtain in this dimension.'

Klandor considered. 'What do you want me to wager in return?'

Watch didn't hesitate. 'Your wizard's hat for the lighter.'

'Is that all?' Klandor asked.

Watch shrugged. 'It's a nice hat. I want it.'

'You want it because it's a magical hat,' Klandor said sternly. 'It is worth far more than your silly lighter.'

'That's my offer. Take it or leave it.'

'I'll make you a counter offer,' the wizard said. 'Both the lighter and the calculator for my hat.'

Watch shook his head. 'No dice.'

Klandor smiled thinly. 'We don't use dice. We toss a coin. Heads or tails. It is very simple. You either win or you lose.' He paused. 'You must wager both.'

'No,' Watch said.

'What are you saving the calculator for?'

'A second wager.'

'What do you want for it?' Klandor asked.

'That is none of your business. Not unless you win both items from me.'

The wizard scowled. 'You are a stubborn human.'

'We are a stubborn race,' Cindy chipped in.

Klandor waved his hand. 'All right, I will put up my hat for the lighter. I will even let you toss the coin, and let you call what you wish while it is still in the air: heads or tails. Does that sound fair?'

'Yes,' Watch replied, bringing out the crystal necklace. 'The only condition I have is that you wear this necklace while we play.'

Every dwarf and elf in the room leaned closer.

Pan smiled faintly although he remained silent.

Klandor was suspicious. Why should I wear it?'

'Why not?' Cindy asked. 'You say it has no effect on the wearer.'

'I must insist that you wear it if you want to win this fine lighter and this superb calculator,' Watch said. 'Our good friend Pan had to wear it before, and now it's your turn.'

'I did not force Pan to wear the necklace,' Klandor said. 'He chose to wear it.'

109

'Is there some reason you are afraid to wear it?' Cindy taunted gently.

The wizard snorted. 'I am afraid of nothing.' He stood from his throne. 'Give me the necklace. Loyal slaves, get my pillow and gold coin.' He rubbed his hands together as if he were eager for the contest to begin. 'Step forward and lay out your goods, Watch. This might be the last time you see them.'

A few minutes later Watch was sitting opposite Klandor, with the whole assembly looking on, many practically holding their breath, the tension was so great. Yet Watch seemed unconcerned as he sat across from the evil wizard. Watch rubbed the gold coin between his fingers.

'Are you sure you don't want to toss it?' Watch asked. 'I don't mind. That way there can be no possibility of my cheating you.' He paused. 'Does that sound fair?'

Klandor grabbed the gold coin from him. 'You think to play with me, young human, but I warn you. I have played against much greater beings than you and I have beaten them every time.'

'Then play. Toss the coin. Call it any way you want.'

Klandor glanced at the coin, at the crystal necklace around his neck, at the crowd. Once more a faint smile touched his lips. He gestured to a nearby dwarf to come closer.

'What is your name?' he asked the dwarf.

'Bartmeal,' the dwarf said.

'Bartmeal,' Klandor said. 'Once the coin lands, I want you to read out what it is to the audience. Heads or tails. You understand?'

The dwarf was uneasy. Obviously he worried that if he had to read out that it was tails, when his master had called for heads, he would be placed in a precarious position. The reverse could be equally compromising. Bartmeal was probably wondering if he would have a head on his shoulders when the day finally ended. Yet he was caught in a jam; there was nothing he could do about it. He seemed resigned. He nodded his large head.

'I understand,' Bartmeal said.

'I want you to tell the truth,' Klandor emphasised.

Bartmeal nodded. 'I will tell the truth, master.'

Watch yawned. 'Can we get on with it please?'

Klandor tossed the coin in the air.

'Tails,' he called out.

It was heads. Bartmeal called out the word.

The assembly buzzed with noise.

Klandor sat astounded. Then he shouted at the group. 'Be quiet!'

The gathering quietened down. Fast.

Klandor reached for his hat and handed it to Watch.

'You have won your prize,' he said in a scratchy voice.

Watch smiled. 'Would you like to win it back? The hat and the lighter? Double or nothing?'

Klandor was interested. His dark eyes flashed with a cold light.

'What do I have to wager?' he asked.

'The freedom of our two friends that you took hostage,' Watch said. 'I assume they are still alive?'

Klandor hesitated. 'Yes, they are alive.' He clapped his hands together. 'Fine, it is a wager. Your friends for my hat and the lighter. But I toss the coin this time as well, and Bartmeal reads out what it is.'

'I would have it no other way,' Watch said.

Klandor tossed the coin in the air.

'Heads!' he called out.

It landed tails. Bartmeal whispered the word to the assembly.

'Louder please,' Cindy called.

'It was tails,' Bartmeal said, throwing his master an anxious look. For his part Klandor fumed.

'You are cheating me,' he accused Watch.

Watch was a picture of innocence. 'How do I cheat you? You control everything.'

Klandor complained. 'I don't know how you are doing it!'

'Is it the necklace?' Watch asked sympathetically. 'Is it disturbing you in some way? I know you made it and everything – in your secret laboratory – but perhaps it is not as safe to wear as you thought. You can take it off now, if you like. I'm sure all those watching wouldn't mind.'

Of course Klandor could not remove the necklace. That would be the same as saying it was somehow crooked, and that Pan had indeed been cheated out of his kingdom. Klandor continued to fret.

'You have to give me a chance to win back what I have lost,' he told Watch.

'Fine. We can go double or nothing again.'

Klandor was wary. 'What do I have to wager?'

'Just your castle.'

'My castle! That's ridiculous. What makes you think I would wager all that just to win a few trinkets and the lives of your friends?'

Watch spoke smoothly, loud enough for all to hear. 'Because you are a gambling wizard. Because you have never lost before. Because you are sure, this time, you can beat me.' Watch paused. 'Or have I really beaten you at your own game?'

The wizard's face flushed with blood. 'I toss the coin again.'

Watch shrugged. 'As you wish.'

Klandor tossed the coin in the air.

'Tails,' he called.

It was heads. Bartmeal didn't look so good.

Nor did Klandor. 'I can't give up my castle,' he moaned.

Watch leaned forward. 'I'll give you a chance to win it back. Double or nothing.'

Klandor sat back. 'What do I have to wager?'

'Everything.'

'What do you mean?'

'Everything you took from Pan: his title, his castle, his kingdom. If you lose you must give it all back.'

Klandor was insulted. 'That's absurd. I would never wager that much.'

'It's your choice,' Watch said.

Klandor burned with indecision. Then he nodded his head vigorously.

'I have to win at least once,' he said.

The wizard tossed the coin in the air.

'Tails!' Klandor screamed.

It was heads. Bartmeal fainted.

Klandor threw a fit. 'I'm not giving up my kingdom!

I'm not going back to being ignored by everyone!'

Pan stepped forward then and grabbed the wizard by the neck.

'You have no coice, Klandor,' he said in a clear, strong voice. 'Just as I had no choice.'

Glancing around the room at the enthusiastic nods of the assembled dwarves and elves, Watch and Cindy could see that everyone else agreed with their old King.

Klandor was history.

But they still needed the wizard for one last hing.

Pan was naturally overjoyed to have his kingdom back, and wanted to throw a huge feast to celebrate. But while they were waiting for the food to be prepared, a rooster and a chicken suddenly flew through the hall. Apparently they had just escaped from the kitchen. Both birds were making an awful noise. Pan nodded to one of the armed elves.

'Shoot those birds down,' he said. 'We can have them with our meal.'

The archer raised his bow and arrow.

'Wait!' Cindy screamed. 'Don't shoot!'

The elf hesitated. Pan looked at Cindy.

'What's the matter?' he asked.

'That's Sally,' she gasped. 'The chicken is Sally.'

'But it's just a chicken,' Watch said.

Cindy shook her head. 'No, it's Sally, I'm positive. The rooster must be Adam. Klandor must have changed them into birds. Pan, we have to get the wizard out of your dungeon. He has to change them back.

'But how can you be so sure?' Pan asked.

Cindy smiled. 'I would recognise that squawk anywhere.'

# Epilogue

Pan was unable to escort them back to the inter-dimensional portal. He said he had too much work to do to get his kingdom in order so that he could invite the elementals now living in Spooksville to come home. Pan wished them his best as they said goodbye, however, and promised that their bikes and other stuff would be returned to them soon.

But cute little fairy Sarshi came along to keep them company. She walked between them as Watch explained his plan to Adam and Sally, who were still scratching at feathers that were no longer there.

'First I reversed the order of the stones in the crystal necklace,' Watch said. 'I discovered that when I did that, it didn't work at all.'

'Then why did you insist Klandor wear it?' Adam asked.

'To confuse him. He expected to see everything the reverse of what he wanted. When that didn't happen during the coin tosses, he lost all balance.'

'But why was that important?' Sally asked.

Watch explained. 'To keep him distracted so that he would not notice that Sarshi was hanging invisible in the air between us, tipping the coin at the last second so that it would always land the opposite of what he called out. I had him throw the coin for that same reason. The more he had to do, the less likely he was to notice what Sarshi was doing.'

Sally patted Watch on the back. 'You're a genius.'

Watch was gracious. 'Cindy contributed at least half the plan.'

'No,' Cindy said. 'Ten per cent, at most.'

Adam patted Cindy on the back. 'You're still a genius.'

Cindy blushed. 'Sarshi deserves most of the credit. After all, she was the one who had to stay invisible right in the face of a powerful wizard, and keep altering the coin as it fell on the pillow. I'm sure that was no easy trick. Isn't that right, Sarshi?'

The little fairy was embarrassed. 'I have a confession to make.'

'What?' Watch asked.

She hesitated. 'I wasn't there.'

Watch chuckled. 'You're kidding.'

'No,' Sarshi said in a tiny voice. 'I couldn't get my invisible web to work. I tried again and again but the spell kept failing.' She added, 'When you were gambling with the wizard, I was sitting in the back with the dwarves, watching.'

They were all shocked.

'But how could you have failed me?' Watch asked.

'Maybe I was too nervous.' She added quietly, 'To tell you the truth, I'm only nine years old.'

Cindy burst out laughing. But Watch was still confused.

'But how did I keep winning every toss?' he asked.

'I don't know.' Sarshi smiled sweetly. 'Sometimes you just get lucky.'

# Spooksville

## THE WISHING STONE

# One

Sally Wilcox saw the Wishing Stone first. For that reason she felt it belonged mainly to her. That was probably the same reason she suffered more than the others from the stone. The more you asked of it, the more it demanded in return. Of course, none of them knew that at first. But even if Sally had known, she probably would have made the same wishes all over again. She was a strong-willed girl, and rather impulsive.

They were not far from Spooksville, their home town, when they came upon the stone. Since dealing with Pan's leprechauns and fairies in the thick forest high in the hills overlooking the town, they had been staying closer to Spooksville, not wandering too deep into the dangerous places that were difficult to get out of. However, no place in or

1

around Spooksville was really safe. The gang was only hiking in the foothills of the foothills when Sally stopped them and pointed toward the sparkle in the trees, some way off their path.

'What's that?' she asked, brushing aside her dark fringe.

'I don't see anything,' Adam Freeman said.

'Neither do I,' Watch said, removing his thick glasses and cleaning them on his shirtsleeve. 'Did you see an animal?'

'No,' Sally said, thoughtful. 'It was just a flash of light.'

'It could just have been a reflection,' Cindy Makey said, standing behind them.

'Obviously,' said Sally, who had been leading the group. 'But a reflection of what?' She paused. 'I think we should take a look.'

'I don't know,' Cindy said, fingering her long blonde hair. 'If we go off the path we'll get our clothes all dirty.'

'And we might run into a strange animal and have our internal organs ripped from our bodies,' Watch added.

Sally frowned at Watch. 'And you used to be so adventurous,' she said.

2

'I was younger then,' Watch said.

'You're only twelve now,' Adam observed. He nodded to Sally. 'I'll go with you and check it out. It shouldn't take long to hike over there.' Sally had pointed to the far side of the gully they were now hiking through.

'We should probably all go together,' Cindy said. 'It's not safe to separate out here.'

'It's not safe to be alive out here,' Sally said.

'But it is better than being dead,' Watch said.

They hiked in the direction of the supposed flash Sally had seen. When they reached the spot, they searched the area without finding anything unusual.

'It was probably just a trick of the light,' Adam said.

'Perhaps some debris from a crashed flying saucer,' Watch added.

But Sally was unconvinced. 'It was a bright flash. There must be something strange out here.'

'But strange is not necessarily good,' Cindy said.

Sally looked at her. 'Are you getting scared again?'

'Yes,' Cindy said sarcastically. 'Just being out in this wilderness with you makes me tremble in my shoes.'

'Let's continue our hike,' said Adam. 'Then we can go and get some ice cream.'

But Sally was unconvinced. 'I want to search the area one more time. I can do it myself. You guys rest here if you're tired.'

In fact, they were all sort of tired. The summer was nearly over, but the sun didn't know that. It was another hot, cloudless day. Adam, Cindy, and Watch plopped down on several boulders in the shade while Sally went off on her own. Cindy had brought a bottle of apple raspberry juice, and passed it around.

'Another ten days and school starts,' Watch said, taking a deep gulp of the juice and letting out a satisfied sigh. 'We won't have many more days like this.'

'We'll have the weekends free,' Adam said. 'We'll have plenty of time to hang out together and have fun.'

Watch shook his head as he passed the juice to Adam. 'You don't know the teachers in this town. They give you so much homework, you have to work on it all weekend just to keep up.'

'Why do they do that?' Cindy said. 'We don't all want to be rocket scientists when we grow up.'

'They just want to give us a chance to complete our studies,' Watch said.

'But what's the hurry?' Adam asked.

Watch shrugged. 'You've been here long enough to know the answer to that. Not that many kids who move here live long enough to graduate. Last year's junior high class graduated only a dozen people, and half of them were missing body parts.'

'What about the other half?' Adam asked reluctantly.

'Most of them were insane,' Watch said.

Cindy grimaced. 'That's horrible!'

'I don't know,' Watch said. 'They had a great all-night leaving party.'

'I hope we get to be in a lot of classes together,' Adam said.

Watch shook his head. 'It might be better to separate. Then, if there is an explosion or something in one of the classes, at least some of us will survive.'

'You have explosions at school?' Cindy asked. 'I don't believe it.'

'We had half a dozen explosions last year. Most of them were in chemistry class. The teacher used to work for the CIA.' Watch added, 'But I think they got rid of him.'

Suddenly they heard Sally shouting.
'I've found something! I've found something!'

# Two

Sally had indeed found an extraordinary object. Nestled between two thick trees and sitting atop a granite boulder was a perfectly-sculpted black hand. It rose right out of the rock, its palm pointed upward toward the sky. Yet the fingers were not completely open; rather, they were slightly clenched around a cube-shaped crystal stone. This crystal was as big as a normal man's hand could comfortably hold, at most five centimetres on each side. Although the nearby trees stood close, a flicker of sunlight occasionally pierced their branches and the stone itself. When this happened there was a bright flash. The stone was clear but it also acted like a mirror, which puzzled Adam.

Now they knew what had caught Sally's eye.

'Isn't it beautiful?' Sally asked, excited.

'Yes,' said Cindy. 'But what is it?'

Adam nodded seriously. 'Good question. And where did it come from? I wonder.' He paused. 'Have you touched it yet, Sally?'

'No. I was waiting for you guys.'

'We might want to leave it alone,' Watch suggested. 'We don't know who it belongs to.'

'It belongs to me,' Sally said. 'I found it.'

'And does every bike you pass on the street belong to you?' Cindy asked. 'Every skateboard? Just because you found something doesn't mean it's yours.'

'It does if you find it in the middle of nowhere,' Sally said, reaching out her hand to pick up the crystal. Adam stopped her.

'Watch is right,' he said. 'We have to be careful.'

Sally was impatient. 'All right, say we take the safe course and talk about this thing for the next hour. In the end we all know that none of us is going to just leave it here for someone else to find. It's too pretty to just leave behind. I say we take it now and be done with it.'

'Hold on.' Adam peered at the black hand, trying to figure out what it was made of. It seemed to be some type of shiny metal, yet when he touched it,

8

the hand felt warm. He told the others.

'Could it be alive?' Cindy whispered.

'It's black,' Watch said. 'If the sun was shining on it that might have made it hot.'

Adam studied the thick overhead trees. 'I don't think the sun made it warm.'

'I don't care about the hand,' Sally said. 'I'm only interested in the crystal.' Again she reached out to take it. 'Don't stop me, Adam.'

None of them stopped her this time, and a second later she was holding the clear cube, rubbing it with her fingers, savouring it as if it was a huge diamond.

'Maybe it is a diamond,' Sally said. 'Maybe I can sell it for ten million dollars.'

'Naturally you would share the profits with us, your best friends,' Cindy said.

Sally snorted. 'You wanted to leave it here. And now that I am holding it and you can see it's safe, you want to make money from it.'

'We reserve judgment at this time as to how safe it is,' Watch said.

'I'm more concerned with who it belongs to,' Adam said. 'I really wish you wouldn't take it, Sally.'

She remained stubborn. 'If anyone reports it missing I will be the first to return it.' She held it up to the sunlight and the crystal sparkled, sending tiny shafts of light into the trees. 'Until then it is mine.'

'Look!' Cindy cried. 'The black hand closed!'

Cindy was right. The palm that had once lightly grasped the crystal was now entirely shut. Apparently the fingers had folded over while they were talking.

'It is alive,' Cindy gasped. 'Quick, Sally, put the crystal back.'

Sally hesitated. 'Just because it moved doesn't mean it's alive.'

'I don't see many of these rocks getting up and doing a dance,' Watch said.

Adam spoke seriously. 'It doesn't belong to you, Sally. To take it is stealing.'

Sally considered. 'All right, I will put it back.' Carefully she held it close to the black hand, thinking it would reach up and grab it. When that didn't happen she tried to push it in between the clenched fingers. But the hand was tightly closed. Finally she gave up. 'It doesn't want it.'

'Then just leave it beside the hand,' Adam

suggested. 'It can reach over and grab it later, if it wants it.'

'No,' Sally said. 'I don't think that's fair. If it wants it, it should take it now.'

'I doubt disembodied black hands understand our concept of fairness,' Watch said.

'I'm not just going to leave it here,' Sally said.

'Thief,' Cindy muttered.

'Coward!' Sally snapped at her.

Adam held up his hands. 'Hold on, let's not have another fight. Maybe we can work out a compromise.'

'There is no compromise,' Sally said. 'I either take it or I don't take it.'

'You could leave a note with your home address on it,' Cindy said. 'That way if the black hand wants it back it can crawl to your house in the middle of the night, choke you to death, and take it back.'

'A novel suggestion,' Watch said.

'We can argue about this all day,' Adam said, resigned to Sally's wishes. 'If you're going to take it, then take it, and let's get out of here.'

'But please walk at least twenty metres behind us,' Cindy said.

'I always walk thirty metres in front of you.' Sally

clasped the crystal to her chest. 'I'm not afraid to go where no woman has gone before.'

They hiked back toward the path. Along the way Sally accidentally stubbed her toe and let out a groan. 'I wish I had a pair of new shoes,' she said, letting the others pass her on the path. 'These are so worn out – they're always hurting my feet.'

Then Sally let out a scream.

They turned anxiously. Sally was so stunned she couldn't even speak. She could only point down. Their eyes took a moment to register why she had screamed. Then it struck them and they let out their own sounds of amazement.

There were brand-new shoes on Sally's feet.

# Three

'It must be a Wishing Stone,' Watch said a few minutes later, after they had all had a chance to catch their breaths. 'Bum has spoken about them before.'

'He has?' Sally asked, still amazed.

Watch nodded. 'He said they could be found on Earth during the Atlantis and Lemuria ages, tens of thousands of years ago. You remember he said that Spooksville was actually once a part of Lemuria. In fact, he says that Spooksville is all that is now left of Lemuria.'

'Did the people at that time make these Wishing Stones?' Adam asked.

Watch was thoughtful. 'Bum didn't go into too many details about them. But I got the impression the stones were put here by extraterrestrial visitors.'

'You mean aliens?' Cindy asked.

'Not necessarily,' Watch said. 'Bum believes this planet was originally colonised by humans from other planets.'

'He mentioned the Pleiades star cluster before,' Adam said. 'Did the Wishing Stones come from there?'

Watch was uncertain. 'He never said one way or the other, not clearly. But I got the impression they were from some place even farther away.'

'Did he say the stones were dangerous?' Cindy asked.

'He laughed when he talked about them, as he usually does when he talks about anything really mysterious,' Watch said. 'I was never sure if they were dangerous or not. But I do know that whoever holds one can ask for whatever he or she wants, and it will instantly appear.' He nodded to Sally's new sneakers. 'But we know that already.'

'Can I ask for as many wishes as I want?' Sally asked.

'I don't think the stones ever run out of power,' Watch said.

Sally squealed with delight. 'Wow! This is absolutely awesome. I'm going to have everything I ever wanted before I turn thirteen.'

'You can get *us* some things too,' Cindy said.

Sally laughed at her. '*Now* you change your mind. *Now* you think I did the right thing.'

Cindy was indignant. 'I just don't think you should be greedy.'

Sally patted her on the back. 'Don't worry, girl, you can have what you want. All I ask is that you be nice to me.'

Watch turned to Adam. 'I think the three of us had better accept what we already have.'

Sally smiled. 'That's not true, I can grant you guys a few wishes. But first I want to get a few things for myself.' She gestured for them to stand back. 'I don't want you crowding my presents.'

'Wait!' Adam said. 'We don't know what these wishes might cost.'

Sally stared at him as if he was nuts. 'Why should they cost me anything? This is a Wishing Stone. It's not a debt collector.'

'But you don't get anything for free in this world,' Adam said.

'But this stone did not come from this world,' Sally said.

'She has a point there,' Watch said.

15

Adam was still worried. 'I think you should be happy with your new pair of shoes and leave it at that.'

Sally laughed again. 'You have to start thinking big, Mr Adam. You don't accept a pair of shoes and walk away when you have the whole world at your fingertips. Now quieten down and let me think what I want.'

'You should get some new clothes,' Cindy suggested.

'Maybe a new watch,' Watch said.

'Shh,' Sally said, closing her eyes and letting her smile grow larger. 'I have something. Yes, this is what I want.' She paused and then blurted out the next words. 'I wish I had a million dollars!'

A million dollars suddenly appeared.

They were one-dollar bills and there were hundreds of stacks, which literally mounted up in piles above their heads. Adam could hardly believe his eyes. Reaching out, he grabbed one of the stacks and studied it. The dollars seemed genuine. Sally squealed again with joy.

'I'm rich!' she said.

'You should have asked for one hundred dollar denominations,' Watch said. 'You're never going to be able to carry this stuff back to your house.'

'Even if you could,' Cindy said. 'You couldn't fit it in your house.'

Sally snickered. 'You're just jealous! I'm a millionaire and you're not.'

'Well maybe you could give us a loan,' Watch said.

'I want some new clothes,' Cindy said suddenly.

'Wait a second,' Adam said. But no one was listening.

'What kind do you want?' Sally asked Cindy.

Cindy rubbed her hands together in expectation. 'I would love a black leather jacket and some black leather boots. Then, I need some clothes for school. How about a sharp Ann Klein suit? Light yellow, with designer buttons and gold-cuffed sleeves.'

'You need this to go to school in Spooksville?' Watch asked.

Sally waved her hand. 'It doesn't matter. If she wants it, she wants it.' Sally closed her eyes, then spoke aloud and wished for exactly what Cindy had just said.

The clothes did not appear.

Sally opened her eyes and studied the stone. 'It can't be broken already. Watch?'

'It's possible Cindy has to make her own wishes,' he said. 'You don't really want these clothes, not the way you wanted the million dollars. Give Cindy the stone and we'll see.'

'I'm not giving her the stone,' Sally said quickly.

'I'll give it back,' Cindy said.

'How do I know you will?' Sally asked in a dangerous voice.

Cindy was insulted. 'When have I ever stolen anything of yours?'

'When have I ever had a Wishing Stone before?' Sally asked.

'This is getting ridiculous.' Adam interrupted. 'This stone is already causing problems. Let's put it back now.'

'There are a couple of things I would like,' Watch said.

Adam was stunned. 'But I thought you agreed with me?'

Watch smiled. 'I did until I saw the million dollars.'

'I will give Watch the stone first,' Sally said. 'As an experiment.'

'What's wrong with me?' Cindy complained.

'Nothing's wrong with you,' Sally said impatiently. 'But I have known Watch longer than you. I know for a fact that he'll give me the stone back when I ask for it.' She went to hand the stone to Watch, and then stopped. 'You will give it back to me, won't you?'

Watch shrugged. 'Sure.'

'Swear on your very life,' Sally ordered.

'It's not good to swear,' Cindy said.

'I swear to whatever you want me to swear to,' Watch said.

'All right.' Sally reluctantly handed over the stone. 'Don't break it.'

Watch held the stone close to his heart and closed his eyes. For a moment he concentrated deeply. Then he spoke. 'I wish for a refractor telescope with clock drive and computer-assisted star finder.'

The telescope appeared just off the path.

'Cool,' Watch said.

'Let me try!' Cindy exclaimed.

'It's my turn,' Sally snapped. 'Watch, give me the stone back.'

'Just a moment,' Watch said, closing his eyes once more. 'I wish for a laser pistol.'

A black pistol-shaped device materialised at his feet.

Watch knelt and picked it up. He pointed it in the direction of a nearby rock and pulled the trigger. There was a flash of red light. The rock exploded into a thousand pieces. The gang jumped, except for Watch. He studied the weapon closer.

'It's interesting,' he muttered.

'It's very powerful,' Adam gasped.

'What I mean,' Watch continued, 'is that the Wishing Stone was able to materialise something that we don't even have on this planet. That's further proof that it must be from another world.'

'I am waiting,' Sally said with her hand outstretched.

'Just a second,' Watch said, closing his eyes once more. 'I wish for the finest portable force shield generator in the entire galaxy.'

A small black oval-shaped object appeared at his feet.

Watch knelt and picked this up as well. There was a series of buttons on the side and he experimented with them for a moment. Then he handed the laser pistol to Adam.

'I want you to shoot me,' he said.

Adam shook his head. 'No way. We don't know

if that force-field generator will protect you. What if it doesn't? You'll die.'

'I have set the laser pistol on stun,' Watch said.

'How do you know for sure?' Adam asked.

'Shoot Sally and see if it knocks her out,' Watch said.

Sally jumped back and held out her hands. 'Don't shoot me! Shoot Cindy!'

Cindy didn't look too happy about the suggestion. 'Don't shoot anybody!' she shouted.

'Shoot a tree then,' Watch said. 'It really is set to stun.'

'You can't stun a tree,' Sally said. 'They're already permanently stunned.'

Nevertheless, Adam turned and shot the nearest tree. Once again a red beam of light shot out, but it left no noticeable impression on the tree bark. Adam decided it was safe enough to fire at his friend.

'You sure you have the force field on?' he asked Watch, taking aim.

'Pretty sure,' Watch said. 'The force field must be invisible. But the worst that can happen is that it knocks me out.'

'You should give me the Wishing Stone first,'

Sally said, moving to retrieve the stone from him. But then she seemed to bump into an invisible wall. She bounced back in mid-stride. Adam and Cindy laughed.

'The force field is definitely working,' Cindy said. 'Watch, you should leave it on all the time.'

'That way Sally will never get the stone back,' Adam added.

'Don't worry,' Watch reassured Sally. 'You will have it back in a second. But stand back right now. Adam, fire away.'

Once more Adam took aim with the laser and fired. The red beam sprayed over a point about half a metre from Watch's body, but it did not touch him. Adam ceased fire and Watch turned off the force field. Adam handed the laser back to his friend. Watch admired the two instruments.

'I've always wanted gadgets like this,' Watch said.

Adam was happy for him, despite his continuing fears about the Wishing Stone. 'I'm sure they will come in handy living in this town,' he said. 'Especially if the Cold People or the demons come back.'

'Thank you very much,' Sally said, snatching the Wishing Stone from Watch's hands. 'You already have more than me, and I found it. Stand back all of you. It is Christmas time in Spooksville.'

'But what about my new clothes?' Cindy asked.

'You'll get those when I'm finished,' Sally said.

She then proceeded to order up new clothes for herself, a new bedroom set, a new TV and stereo, and another million dollars – in one hundred dollar denominations. But when Cindy finally got her hands on the Wishing Stone she didn't hold back: more clothes, a new bike, hundreds of CDs, boxes of books. Soon the path was littered with so much it would take a couple of large trucks to haul it all away. Adam said as much.

'Most of this is just going to go to waste out here,' he said. 'You should have at least made your wishes back in town.'

'We can bring the stuff back piece by piece,' Sally said, stuffing her pockets with one hundred dollar bills. 'That reminds me, Adam. What do you want?'

Adam shook his head. 'Nothing.'

Sally held out the Wishing Stone. 'Come on, don't try to be a moralist. At least get yourself some new clothes. You look like your mother dresses you.'

Adam was insulted. 'My mother does buy all my clothes.'

'There you go,' Cindy said, trying on a new sweater over her tee shirt.

Adam was even more insulted. 'You really think I dress like a nerd?'

'I didn't say the nerd word,' Cindy said quickly.

'But she was obviously thinking it,' Sally said, still holding out the stone for him to take. 'Improve your image, Adam, what can it hurt?'

'You might want to get yourself a laser pistol,' Watch said. 'We could play war games together.'

Adam reluctantly accepted the Wishing Stone. 'I'm not going to wish for anything for myself,' he said.

'But it only works if you really want what you're wishing for,' Cindy said.

'I can really want something and it doesn't have to be for myself,' Adam said. Holding the Wishing Stone tightly, he closed his eyes and said, with as much feeling as possible, 'I wish for galactic peace.'

Nothing happened, of course. Nothing that they could see. The others stared at him as if he had lost his mind.

'What good is a wish like that?' Sally asked.

Adam shrugged. 'It's something I would like. For everybody to live in peace.'

'Wasn't world peace big enough for you?' Watch asked.

'We've been talking about people on other planets,' Adam said. 'Why should I leave them out?'

'But get something for yourself,' Cindy said. 'A new skateboard at least.'

'Yeah,' said Watch. 'You're making the rest of us feel guilty.'

But Adam handed the Wishing Stone back to Sally. 'Maybe later,' he said. 'I don't feel like I need anything right now.'

For the time being that settled that discussion. They spent the next ten minutes trying to figure out how much they could carry back to town. Even though it was a warm day, Cindy had gone behind a bush and dressed herself in *two* new outfits at once. Sally seemed preoccupied mainly with carrying away as much cash as possible. And Watch quickly discovered he couldn't move his telescope very far, and ended up only taking the laser pistol and the portable force field generator with him. For his part, Adam helped Cindy with her new bike.

'Next I'm going to wish for a gold credit card,'

Sally said as she skipped in front of them with the Wishing Stone in her hand.

# Four

They were ten minutes on the way home when a dark figure in a red robe appeared on the path in front of them. He was hooded; the shadow cast by his hood made his face a black well of mystery. But in the shadow two eyes glittered with wicked red light. He was tall and his arms were exceptionally long. He raised a hand as they stood stunned by his sudden appearance. It was only then that they realised his hands were identical to the one on the granite boulder where they had found the Wishing Stone.

'I am the Collector,' he said in a strangely mechanical voice. 'I am here to collect on your debt.'

'I was worried something like this would happen,' Adam muttered.

'This character surpasses the worst worry I had,' Sally whispered, fear in her voice. 'What are we going to do?'

'Maybe you could give him some of your cash,' Cindy said anxiously.

'I don't think this guy can be bought off,' Watch said.

'Let me try talking to him,' Adam said, taking a shaky step forward. He waved to the dark figure and cleared his throat. 'Hi, my name's Adam Freeman and these are my friends. What exactly is this debt you're talking about?'

The dark figure lowered his right hand and a metallic scroll appeared in it. He read from it in his peculiar steel voice. It did not sound as if he was a living creature at all, but something built in an alien laboratory.

'Sara Wilcox – ten thousand and sixty-four gratoms,' he said. 'Cynthia Makey – one thousand and eighty-two gratoms. Watch – nine hundred and forty-one gratoms. Adam Freeman – you owe . . .' The dark figure trailed off for a moment. 'Your debt has yet to be added up, but it looks as if it will be large.' He paused. 'These were all placed on the same order.'

'This is from the stuff we wished for with the Wishing Stone?' Adam asked.

'Yes. The debt is due immediately and must be paid in full.'

'We did not know that,' Adam said.

'It does not matter. I am the Collector. I am here to collect your debts. Now.'

'Ask if we can just give the stuff back,' Cindy suggested.

'Maybe not all of it back,' Sally muttered.

'Can we just pay off the debt by returning the goods?' Adam asked.

'There is no refund policy. Your debts are due immediately. Hand over the gratoms now.'

'But we don't have any gratoms,' Watch said. 'We don't even know what they are.'

The Collector moved his fingers and the metallic scroll vanished. In its place was a small spherical object lined with numerous glowing buttons and flashing lights. It seemed to hum as it sat in the Collector's hand, filling each of them with an ominous feeling.

'The debt must be paid immediately,' the Collector said in his robotic voice. 'If you cannot pay then each of you must work off the debt on a slave planet.'

Adam held up a hand. 'Now wait a second. This is not fair. This Wishing Stone was just sitting in the middle of nowhere. No instructions came with it. There wasn't even a warning label on the side. We can't be responsible for debts we had no idea we were getting into.'

'I am a Collector,' the dark figure repeated. 'I am here to collect your debts. I do not argue over how you accumulated these debts. And since you have made it clear that you have no gratoms to pay for these debts, you will now be transported to a slave planet where you will spend the rest of your lives working off these debts.' He fiddled with the controls on the sphere in his hands. 'Stand ready to be transported to Amacron 37.'

'Wait!' Adam pleaded. 'We're not ready to be transported anywhere. We need to talk about this some more.'

'We should at least be allowed to talk to a lawyer,' Sally said, stepping forward and pointing an angry finger at the Collector. 'You show up here and say you're a Collector and we have to pay you and everything. How do we know you're not a fake? You haven't even shown us ID. You haven't even . . .'

Sally was cut off in mid sentence.

There was a flash of green light. It came from the sphere.

And Sally was gone. Just gone.

'On no,' Cindy cried.

There was another flash of green light.

Then Cindy was gone.

'Get out of the way, Adam!' Watch shouted.

Adam wasn't even given a chance to think. He dived to the side of the path. This time there was a burst of red light. Adam felt for sure he was on his way to some forsaken slave world. But then the Collector collapsed on the path and the transporting sphere rolled lazily into the bushes. Out the corner of his eye Adam saw Watch lowering his laser pistol.

'I wish I was a faster draw,' Watch said.

Adam understood. They had lost the girls. Adam stood and brushed off his trousers. Together they stepped to where the Collector had fallen. He lay face down, covered in his hood. Watch reached down and felt for a pulse at the Collector's neck, then jerked his hand back.

'I think I killed him,' he whispered. 'But the laser was set to stun.'

Adam shook his hand. 'I don't think this guy

was ever alive. You heard his mechanical voice. He's a robot.'

Watch stood and nodded grimly. 'You're probably right. Maybe the stun was enough to destroy his positronic brain.' He pointed to the sphere that had rolled into the bushes. 'I wonder if we can figure how to use that.'

Adam picked it up. Although small, there must have been at least twenty controls on the object. 'It would take a genius to understand how to operate it.'

'I'm supposed to have a genius IQ,' Watch said. 'Give it to me.'

Adam handed it over. 'What is your IQ?'

'One hundred and sixty.'

'I'm impressed.'

'I try not to brag about it,' Watch said.

While Watch was examining the device Adam studied the places where Cindy and Sally had disappeared. There were no burn marks on the ground, nothing to show that they had been beamed away to another planet. Amacron 37 – it sounded awfully far from home to Adam. He was about to turn back to Watch when a flash of light in the nearby grass caught his eye.

Sally had dropped the Wishing Stone.

Adam brought it over to Watch. 'It must have fallen from her hand during the transportation process,' Adam said.

'We might want to order up a few more laser pistols before the Collector's pals come looking for him,' Watch said.

'I think that will just bring his pals quicker.' Adam gestured to the fallen Collector, who had yet to move an inch. 'I don't think we have all that much time. Have you been able to figure out how it works?'

'I know how to turn it on. I watched the Collector when he zapped Sally and Cindy. But that is not the same as knowing how to operate it.'

'Maybe we don't have to know everything. The settings should be the same as when the Collector zapped the girls. If we zap ourselves, we should go to the same place.'

Watch was doubtful. 'Maybe.'

'We have to give it a try.'

Watch hesitated. 'Do we want to do that? I mean, that slave labour planet didn't sound like a relaxing vacation spot.'

'We have no choice. If we don't save the girls, who will?'

'If we can't save the girls, who's going to save us?'

Adam was astounded. 'I can't believe you would leave the girls to suffer lives of torment and misery.'

'I didn't say that was my first choice. I was just reviewing all our options.'

'What other option do we have?' Adam asked.

'We could go home and pretend none of this ever happened.' Watch stopped and scratched his head. 'But I don't suppose we would be able to live with that decision.' He gestured Adam closer. 'Get right beside me. I'll try to zap us both at the same time. That might increase the odds we go to the same place.'

Adam pressed up against his side and stared at the mysterious sphere, which Watch held at arm's length. 'What if it beams us into deep space?' he asked.

'Then we will have a hard time catching our breath.'

'Should we bring the Wishing Stone with us?'

'Yes,' Watch said, his finger on the purple button. 'We might be wishing for a couple of space suits in the next ten seconds.'

'I knew you were going to say that,' Adam replied, stuffing the stone in his pocket.

Watch pushed the button and the Earth vanished.

# Five

Amacron 37 was desolate and miserable. A desert planet with two yellow moons and a purple sun, the wind blew thin and dry fifteen hours a day, which was the length of Amacron 37's day. Yet the air was not particularly hot – just unsatisfying. The world was obviously old and burnt out – there was hardly enough oxygen to support life. When Sally and Cindy first materialised on the planet, they wondered if they would survive the night.

There was no transition for them. They were on the path with Adam and Watch – and the Collector – and the next moment they were being herded toward a desolate barracks by a couple of steel robots with electric sticks. When the sticks touched you, they gave you a sharp jolt. Yet the girls did not argue with the robots or put up a fight, although

Sally was given a shock once just for stumbling on the sand. The voltage was not excessively high, but the stick did hurt. Basically they were in too much confusion to do anything much except what they were told.

The inside of the barracks was dusty and dark. They were shown to a couple of hard bunks and told to rest until the morning shift. Apparently they had been transported at the end of the work day, although the tiny purple sun was still in the sky, along with the two tired moons. Glancing around the dim barracks, they could see that not all the inhabitants were humanoid. There were a couple of huge bear-like creatures and one who seemed to be a cross between a spider and an overgrown butterfly. Everyone else seemed to be resting. No one stood to greet them, other than the two steely robots. One of the robots gestured with its electric stick.

'You will be called to labour in five zomas,' it said.

'How long is a zoma in human hours?' Sally asked.

'Forty minutes,' the robot said, and turned away with his companion.

Sally and Cindy sat on their respective bunks. They had left home only minutes ago but they already had sand in their ears from the short walk outside. Both looked as miserable as they felt.

'I wonder where the boys are?' Sally said finally.

'Maybe they were transported to another planet,' Cindy said.

'The Collector implied that we were all going to Amacron 37.' Sally paused. 'Maybe they escaped somehow.'

'I doubt it. They were probably just transported to another part of this planet.'

Sally was thoughtful. 'Watch had the laser pistol. Maybe he blew the Collector away.'

'Even if he did, I don't think that's going to help us at all.'

Sally sighed. 'All that good stuff isn't any use here.'

Cindy agreed. 'You would have thought they would at least have let us bring it with us. It looks like we'll be paying for it for a long time.'

A soft voice spoke near them. 'You only get what you wished for after you finish paying off your debts.'

They looked over at the neighbouring bunk. A

girl who appeared to be their age, with a green face and white eyes, sat up on her bunk and studied them. Her hair was long and black, so curly it looked as if it would be longer than she was if you straightened it all out. Yet she was beautiful, even with a green face, even by human standards. Plus her voice was a thing of music, gentle and melodious.

'Who are you?' Sally asked.

'My name is Hironee. What are your names?'

'I'm Sally and this is Cindy.' Sally paused. 'Have you been here long?'

Hironee was grave. 'Half my life. I assume you are both from Earth?'

'Yeah,' Cindy said. 'You've heard of the place?'

'I had a friend who was from there. His name was Charles. It was he who taught me your language. Except for the local boss and the robots – who know every language in the galaxy – I am the only one on Amacron 37 who knows English.'

'But what happened to Charles?' Cindy asked.

Hironee spoke sadly. 'He had been here for five years and then one day he just couldn't take it any more. He tried to escape.' Hironee lowered her head. 'The robots caught him in the deep desert, and burned him to a crisp.'

'Has anyone ever escaped from here?' Sally asked.

Hironee glanced up. 'There are stories that a few have escaped, over the last ten thousand years. But no one has got away while I have been here. This particular camp is surrounded by an invisible force field. Even to get out into the deep desert, you have to disable to force field. Charles did that by making a bomb out of local chemicals in the soil. But then there is nowhere to go in the desert. Either the elements kill you or the robots find you and cut you down with their lasers.'

'What planet are you from?' Cindy asked.

Hironee brightened. 'My planet is named Zanath. It is very beautiful, littered with what you would call tropical islands. I was very happy there.' She added wistfully, 'I miss it very much.'

'Were you brought here by a Collector?' Sally asked.

'Yes. I accidentally found a Wishing Stone and made a few wishes on it before the Collector appeared and demanded I pay him five hundred and sixteen gratoms.'

'Exactly how long have you been here?' Sally asked.

'Four of your years.'

'How many gratoms have you worked off in that time?'

'Three gratoms,' Hironee said, when she laughed softly, although it was a sad laugh. 'It really doesn't matter what your debt is. You will never pay it off before you die. That's the way the Kasters set up the system.'

'That's what I suspected,' Sally said grimly.

'Who are the Kasters?' Cindy asked.

'They are the ones who construct the Wishing Stones. They seed them on planets all over the galaxy, and use them to ensnare slave labour. The more advanced civilisations are aware of them and never use the stones. But the Kasters are always finding fresh slaves to work for them. They are shady businessmen, a greedy race of reptiles with a ruthless reputation for cheating and extortion. They also construct the robots who run this slave planet and many others like it.'

'Are there any Kasters here?' Sally asked.

'One. His name is Teeh, and he is horrible. He is the one I told you about who also speaks English. You'll meet him tomorrow – he goes out of his way to harass new slaves.' Hironee lowered her voice.

42

'Don't ever anger him. He'll peel the skin off your body and eat it in front of you. I've seen him do it before.'

'Why don't the more advanced civilisations in the galaxy stop the Kasters from taking slaves?' Cindy asked.

'The Kasters are a powerful and feared race. They only take slaves from those who have become indebted to them. This is what you would call a loophole in the galactic law. It allows them to operate just outside the law. Plus a lot of races still buy Kaster goods. There is always a market from them and some races prefer to keep the market open. Here on this planet you will make Kaster lamps for the rest of your lives.' Hironee shrugged. 'They're pretty good lamps. They last longer than us.'

'We will not be remaining here for the rest of our lives,' Sally said flatly. 'We are going to escape. I don't care how long it takes but I will not stay here and make lamps for a bunch of slimy reptiles.'

Hironee cautioned Sally to lower her voice. She glanced around the barracks, her white eyes glittering in the dark.

'Be careful what you say. Teeh has spies

everywhere. We can talk about such matters during the work shift when not so many ears are so close. But I can tell you now that it is better, in the long run, to accept your situation and try to live with it. There is no real chance of escape. Remember what happened to Charles.'

Sally lowered her voice to a whisper. 'Cindy and I are from Spooksville. It's the roughest town on Earth. You may have heard about it from Charles. It's prepared us for places like this. I don't want to brag about our past, but let's just say we have been in worse fixes than this before.'

'We have?' Cindy said.

Sally continued as if she hadn't heard her. 'Cindy and I are intelligent and resourceful kids. We will never accept this situation.' Sally glanced out the barracks window at the setting purple sun. 'The Kasters are going to regret they ever brought us here.'

# Six

Adam and Watch materialised underground in a huge rocky cavern. The place was far from empty but their sudden appearance didn't even cause a stir. There had to be a hundred different kinds of races milling about the cavern. It seemed to be a marketplace of sorts. There were creatures of every colour and shape – some looked more like monsters than intelligent beings, especially the insectile beings. Adam shuddered as a couple walked close by and stared at them with several hundred emotionless eyes.

'Those two look like they would like to have us for dinner,' Adam muttered.

'Yeah,' Watch said. 'I think we had better get off this platform. It's probably where people beam into this place.'

They headed into the corner of the cavern, in the direction of what looked like a food place. There were numerous tables set up and people were feasting on an exotic array of dishes. In between the tables squat robots with square heads took orders and delivered the meals.

'Do you think this is Amacron 37?' Adam asked.

'No,' Watch said without hesitation. 'This is not a slave planet. All these people look like they're out for a pleasant afternoon of shopping.'

'But why should the transporter send us to another planet?'

'You forget that the Collector dropped the sphere as he fell,' Watch explained, still holding the instrument in his right hand. He had tucked the laser in his belt, under his shirt. 'A button was probably pushed that moved the destination control to the next place on the list.'

'Makes sense. But maybe someone here can tell us how to set the sphere for the slave planet.'

'We might want to find out about the place before we go barging in,' Watch said, finally putting the sphere in his front pocket.

Adam nodded. 'Good idea.' He pointed to the

far corner. 'Let's sit at that table over there and act like we belong here.'

They were not seated long when one of the short robots with a square head approached and wanted to take their order. It looked like a box of metal on wheels, except for its mouth, which faintly resembled a human mouth with a serious case of braces. It nodded as it approached and then gestured with an aluminium-coloured arm for them to speak, probably to find out what planet they were from and what language they spoke. They worked this out because right after Adam and Watch said hello, it replied in a clear, mechanical voice:

'Earth. English.'

'That's correct,' Watch said. 'You speak English?'

'Fluently. What would you two sentient beings like to eat and drink?'

Adam glanced at Watch. 'We don't have any gratoms. We better not order anything.'

'There is no charge for these services,' the robot interrupted. 'What would you like to eat and drink?'

Watch removed his thick glasses and cleaned them on his shirt. 'What do you have?' he asked.

'To repeat verbally our complete menu in the English language would take a long time,' the robot said. 'But we do have a wide variety of Earth dishes. Perhaps you could order and I will tell you if we can meet your needs.'

Adam brightened. 'Could I have a turkey sandwich on white toast, with lettuce and tomato, no mayonnaise? And an order of French fries and a large Coke?'

'Certainly,' the robot said. He turned to Watch. 'And you, sir?'

'I would like a pepperoni pizza with a large Coke.'

'Is that all?'

'Bring us a bag of chocolate chip cookies as well,' Watch said.

The robot was agreeable. 'Your order will take ten earth minutes to prepare. But I can bring your drinks within two minutes.' The robot turned to leave.

'Excuse me,' Adam said. 'Just before you go. What planet is this?'

'This is not a planet, sir, but an asteroid. Its name is Globar 92.'

'Are we far from Amacron 37?' Watch asked.

'Yes. Two thousand seven hundred and eighteen point six light years.'

'Thank you,' Adam said. 'My friend and I will have ice with our Cokes.'

The robot left and Watch nodded seriously. 'I suspected we were on an asteroid. Notice that this whole place is underground?'

'Yeah. But at least it's nice how you don't have to pay for lunch.'

'We should wait until we get our food to see how nice it is.'

But Watch's concerns proved groundless. The food – when it arrived – was very good. The Cokes, in fact, tasted identical to Earth's, but the robot explained that they were popular even in this part of the galaxy. Adam wolfed down his sandwich. Fighting with mysterious forces always made him hungry.

It was while they were eating their cookies that the stranger arrived. One moment they were alone and the next he was standing beside their table.

'May I join you?' he asked. But those were not exactly the words that came from his mouth. He spoke another language, but a voice box clipped to his belt provided them with the translation. Indeed, he had two extra boxes with him, which he quickly offered to Adam and Watch. Apparently they were universal translators that were often employed in such places as Globar 92. Adam and Watch clipped them to their own belts.

'Sure,' Adam said, as the box translated his word into the visitor's language. 'You can sit down.'

'But before you do we would prefer you to tell us what you want,' Watch said.

Adam could see Watch's point. The guy would have stood out at a Hallowe'en party. He was ghastly thin and white as a bed-sheet. His features were human as far as shape and function were concerned, but his eyes were completely blue, as was his long robe. To top it off he was smoking a fat cigar, and he didn't have a trace of hair on his body. On the crown of his head he wore a square blue cap. He blew cigar smoke in Watch's direction as Watch's comment was translated by the box translators on their belts.

'My name is Fur,' he said. 'I am well known in these parts. Ask anybody about me, they'll give me a good recommendation.'

'What would they recommend you for?' Adam asked.

'I am a trader,' Fur said. 'I make deals, good deals. May I sit down?'

'Yes,' Adam said. 'I'm Adam and this is Watch.'

'Pleased to meet you both.'

'Why are you called Fur?' Watch asked. 'You look as if you don't have a hair on your body.'

Fur appeared displeased as he pulled up a chair. 'Is it the custom on your world to insult somebody because they are bald?' He stroked his shiny white head. 'When I get a little ahead, I plan to have a hair transplant.'

'Where are they going to transplant it from?' Watch asked. 'Your twin sister?'

'Fur,' Adam said quickly. 'My friend doesn't mean to be rude. We're just curious about what you want.' He added, 'We're strangers to these parts.'

'I can see that,' Fur said. 'I spotted you the moment you came in, and have been studying you since.' He paused. 'I know you're from Earth, and that you're young by that society's standards.'

'We're not that young,' Watch said.

Fur smiled and they saw that his teeth were blue as well. 'I am not bald and you are not young. Very well, we are off to a good start.' He leaned closer and lowered his voice. The translator softened as well – it was clearly capable of distinguishing different emotional tones. 'I couldn't help noticing that you came in carrying a Kaster transporter.'

'We did?' Adam asked. 'I mean, yeah, so what? It's a good make.'

Fur's smile broadened. 'The Kaster do not sell their transporters, not willingly. I can only assume you obtained this one through – how should I put it – unusual means.'

Watch shrugged. 'I don't see what business that is of yours.'

Fur shrugged. 'I am not interested in how you got it. I just want to know if you want to sell it.'

'No,' Watch said.

'Don't you want to know what I would give you for it?' Fur asked.

'No,' Watch said.

Adam raised a hand. 'Just a second, Watch. Let's listen and see what's available.' He paused. 'What are you offering, Mr Fur?'

'Just call me Fur. I can offer you pretty much whatever you want.' He laughed out loud. 'You really should ask around about me. They'll tell you that there's nothing Fur can't get you, and quick.'

'Except perhaps a Kaster transporter,' Watch said.

Fur lost his smile. 'They are not easily available,

it is true. But come, name your price. I am willing to bargain.'

'Can you give us twenty thousand gratoms?' Watch asked.

Fur blinked. 'You can't be serious? I don't have that kind of wealth. There isn't a sentient being in this place who does. What's the matter? Do you owe a Kaster Collector a Wishing Stone debt?'

Adam hesitated. 'As a matter of fact we do.'

Fur nodded, taking it all in. 'And the Collector appeared and tried to collect the debt. And somehow you two destroyed the Collector and took its transporter. I see the whole picture now. Am I right?'

'You're close,' Adam admitted. 'Before we could take care of the Collector, it managed to transport two of our friends to Amacron 37.' He added, 'That's Sally and Cindy. I don't suppose you've heard of them?'

Fur was grave. 'I have not heard of them nor will they ever be heard from again. If they have gone to a Kaster slave planet, there is no escape for them. They are doomed to work like slaves for the remainder of their lives.'

'Sally always was a good worker,' Watch said,

trying to put a positive spin on the matter. But Adam was appalled.

'There must be some way to save them,' he said.

Fur shook his head. Apparently that was still 'no' in that part of the galaxy.

'The Kaster keep perfect records,' he explained. 'They never allow a debt to go unpaid. That is the cornerstone of their ruthless reputation. Even if you could somehow break into Amacron 37 – which would be next to impossible – they would still have a record of your friend's debts. They would hunt them down to the last corner of the galaxy and make them pay.'

'Where are these records kept?' Watch asked.

Fur had to think. 'In various places. For Amacron 37 I imagine the records are stored on Tallas 4. That's the Orion sector. But you don't want to go there.'

'Why not?' Adam asked.

Fur wrinkled his nose. 'They have lousy food.'

Adam and Watch looked at each other.

'Is there another reason we can't go to Tallas 4, beside the lousy food?' Adam asked.

'Lots of reasons,' Fur said. 'The place is a heavily-fortified moon. Get within half a light year of it and the Kaster will blow you out of the sky.' He paused. 'Why would you want to go there?'

'Isn't it obvious?' Adam asked. 'We want to erase the record of our friends debts.'

Fur snorted. 'That isn't going to happen.'

Adam spoke in a stern voice. 'If it doesn't happen you're not going to get our Kaster transporter.'

Once again Fur lost his smile. 'I can't take you to Tallas 4. Even my wonderful ship – the *Fruitfly* – doesn't have a force field capable of withstanding what they would hit us with.'

'But what if you had a Kaster force field surrounding your ship?' Watch asked.

Fur was instantly interested. 'You have such a device?'

'We have a portable force field generator,' Adam said quickly. 'We don't know if that can protect your ship.'

'If it's the one I'm thinking of it can protect a whole battleship.' Fur stuck out his white hand. 'Let me see it.'

Watch hesitated. 'How do we know you will give it back once we hand it over?'

'Because if I cheated you here, in front of all these

people, my reputation would be permanently ruined. Don't worry, Watch. I just want to check its serial number.'

Watch took out the oval-shaped generator and gave it to Fur, who studied it intently. Apparently the serial number was not something you read on the side of the object. But finally Fur's face brightened.

'You must have wished for the top of the line,' he exclaimed.

'Naturally,' Watch said.

Fur continued. 'The size of the field can be adjusted to accommodate the *Fruitfly*. The field can even be altered so that it makes my ship temporarily invisible. But that does not mean that we can simply break into Tallas 4 and erase all the Kaster records. To do that we would have to blow up their computers, and that would take heavy fire power.'

Watch pulled out the laser pistol. 'Would this help?'

Fur was not impressed. 'You didn't ask for the top of the line there. That's a beryllium laser. They're dependable but nothing special.'

'Why can't we just beam ourselves to Tallas 4

using the Kaster transporter?' Adam asked.

'Tallas 4 is shielded, as is Amacron 37. You cannot transport through a shield. You need to take a ship, and then the ship has to either sneak by the shield with a Kaster vessel, or else break through it directly.' Fur shook his head. 'Either way the chances of success are not good. Why don't I give you something else for the transporter and the force field generator? I'd like them both. How about I give you my own house? I own an asteroid in the Taurus quadrant. You have great views of the Milky Way there, and the home-owner association charges are reasonable.'

'Sounds like a workable deal,' Watch said.

'No,' Adam exclaimed. 'We have to rescue our friends. You either help us save them or there's no deal.'

Fur smiled thinly. 'If I help you, I will probably end up as dead as you will end up. That doesn't sound like a good deal to me.'

'It's the only deal we have to offer you,' Adam said. 'Take it or leave it.'

'Are you sure I couldn't interest you in a couple of Sirian pleasure robots? You can have them designed to your own specifications.'

'We are too young to have girlfriends,' Watch said.

'But Sally and Cindy are still very important to us,' Adam added. 'Even if they aren't real girlfriends.'

Fur considered. 'You would have to give me both the Kaster transporter and Kaster force field generator. I wouldn't take one item.'

'Fine,' Adam said. 'As long as you take us back to Earth after we wreck the Kaster records and rescue the girls.'

Fur frowned and puffed on his cigar. 'Are you sure you want to go back home? The food's lousy there as well.' He added, 'Except for your Cokes. I can drink six of those in a day.'

'Do we have a deal?' Adam asked.

Fur hesitated. 'We'll probably all die. I wasn't kidding.'

Adam stuck out his hand. 'Do we have a deal?'

Fur glanced around and then finally offered his hand. 'I have a feeling I'm going to regret this,' he said.

# Seven

The work shift on Amacron 37 was hard. First they were treated to a breakfast of cold, soggy porridge, and then they were herded into a stark warehouse where the Kaster lamps were assembled. Sally and Cindy were handed a welding gun and dark goggles and told to get to work. A supervising robot stood not far away, its electric stick held ready to shock those who were slow on the job. Cindy held up her welding gun.

'I don't know how to use this,' she said.

'We better figure out quick or scrap metal over there is going to light us up like a Christmas tree,' Sally said.

Fortunately Hironee appeared right then. The way she carried her welding gun, she looked like an expert. 'They have put you on the easy duty,' she explained, pointing to the half-finished lamps in front of them. They were big by human standards, made of very dark metal, very unattractive. 'You just have to weld the lower four joints into place. A child can do it.'

'That's good because we are only kids,' Cindy said, feeling anxious.

Hironee turned and spoke to the closest robot. 'I am going to show the humans how to perform their duties efficiently. Is that acceptable?'

'Efficient work is always acceptable,' the robot replied.

'You just have to know how to talk to a robot,' Hironee said, striking up the arc on her welding gun and pulling her dark goggles over her eyes. She bent down over the lamp in front of Sally. 'You have to make sure that the joint is firmly welded before you go on to the next one. Watch.'

While Hironee worked, the girls stood at her back and spoke in low tones. Sally did most of the talking.

'How many robots are there in this particular camp?' she asked.

'Twenty,' Hironee replied, the sparks of the welding gun spraying not far from her green face.

'And there's Teeh, who watches over them and us.'

'The reptilian Kaster?' Sally asked.

'Yes. He's worse than a dozen robots put together.'

'Do the robots have separate brains?' Sally asked. 'Or are they all controlled from a central place?'

'Both,' Hironee said. 'They have individual positronic brains, but they can be shut down from the computer in Teeh's office. But don't even dream of getting in there. It's heavily guarded.'

'Is the force field that surrounds this camp controlled from there?' Sally asked.

'Yes.'

'Did Charles bomb Teeh's office? Is that how he got through the force field?'

Hironee glanced behind them at the watching robot. 'No. He bombed the field generator itself. If he had been able to bomb the office, the robots wouldn't have caught him so quick and killed him. The computers would have crashed and the robots would have been disabled. But you must stop this line of thinking. I told you, no one can even get close to Teeh's office.'

Sally turned to Cindy. 'We have to get in there. We have to disable the computer. It's the only way.'

'But Hironee says that's impossible,' Cindy protested.

'Do you want to stay here?' Sally demanded.

'No,' Cindy said. 'But I don't want to die either. Besides, even if we are able to flee into the desert, what are we going to do out there?'

'Adam and Watch will come for us,' Sally said simply.

Cindy shook her head. 'You're dreaming. They're on another part of the planet. Their situation is as lousy as ours.'

'Hironee,' Sally said. 'If friends of ours were being sent here at the same time as us, would they have come here?'

'Were their wishes all placed on the same order?'

'Yes,' Sally said. 'The Collector specified that.'

'The they probably would have come here. But . . .' Hironee hesitated.

'What?' Cindy asked.

'If they resisted transportation they might have been killed back on Earth.'

Cindy's lower lip quivered. 'Oh no. That's probably what happened.'

'Nonsense,' Sally said impatiently. 'A single Collector could not take out Adam and Watch. I'm

62

sure Watch was able to shoot him with his laser. Then they probably took the transporter device. I bet they're on their way here now.'

Hironee stopped welding and glanced up. 'I told you, this place is shielded. They couldn't transport here. They would have come in on a ship, a powerful ship.'

'But if we escape from this camp,' Sally said, 'they would be able to pick us up in the desert?'

'*If* you can escape here,' Hironee said. '*If* they are coming to your rescue. But those are two big ifs. You can't risk your life on them.'

'I would rather die than be a slave for the rest of my life,' Sally said.

Hironee cautioned them to be silent. 'Teeh is coming,' she said.

The Kaster boss was as ugly as his reputation. He looked like a crocodile that had one day decided to stand up on his hind legs. His thick tail flapped all over the place as he strode into the warehouse. He had a long snout and large dripping teeth. He wore silver-coloured armoured plate over his chest. But the worst thing were the sunglasses he sported at the end of his snout. For some reason they disturbed the girls more than anything else, possibly because they were cheap sunglasses. He waddled over to where they stood.

'Are you the new slaves?' he asked in a slobbery voice.

'Yes, sir,' Cindy said, standing stiffly, worried about having her skin peeled off and eaten in front of her.

'We are Sally and Cindy,' Sally said. 'I am Sally.'

'I am Cindy,' Cindy said.

'How come you're not working?' he demanded.

'I was just showing them how to use the welding gun, sir,' Hironee said.

Teeh was annoyed. 'Did I ask you? Was I talking to you?'

'No sir,' Hironee said, lowering her head.

'We just got here,' Sally said.

'I know that,' Teeh said. 'Do you think I'm blind? I know everybody here.' He leaned closer and studied Sally. 'Where are the other two?'

'Which other two?' Cindy asked.

'Your two friends,' Teeh said. 'Adam Freeman and Watch. They made wishes as well. I sent the Collector to fetch all four of you. Where are they?'

Cindy shrugged. 'We don't know.'

'I know,' Sally said suddenly.

'Where?' Teeh asked, losing his patience.

Sally looked around as if they were being spied on. 'I can't tell you here. We'd better talk in your office.' She added, 'It's a long story and the information could put your position in danger.'

Teeh frowned, as best a standing crocodile can. 'How can I be in danger?'

Sally leaned closer and spoke in his ear. 'Only I can tell you. I am here to help you.'

'Why should you, a human, help me?'

'Because I want to get ahead here,' Sally said. 'I don't mind stabbing my own people in the back.'

Teeh stepped back and looked around as well. She had sized him up correctly; he was very paranoid, and yet understood greedy ambition.

'Come with me to my office,' he ordered and turned away.

Hironee looked at Sally with worried eyes as she was led away. 'Be careful, Sally.'

'I know what I'm doing,' Sally whispered in reply. But she looked scared.

# *Eight*

They were in deep space, a few hours away from Globar 92, with so many stars around that Adam felt as if he fallen into an alien's dream. The *Fruitfly* was not a large ship – the control room was no bigger than Adam's bedroom. The ceiling of the control room was clear as glass, as was the large viewing screen that Fur sat before. When Fur dimmed the lights it was easy to believe they were floating free in space without protective walls around them. Yet Adam found the sensation exhilarating, as he did Fur's explanation of how they would get to Tallas 4.

'We have to move there through a series of hyperjumps,' Fur said as Watch and Adam listened closely. 'Hyperspace is a region where the three dimensions of normal space can be folded in virtually no space. It makes interstellar travel possible. Without hyperjumps it would take centuries to journey between the stars.'

'Why do we have to make a series of jumps?' Watch asked. 'Why not just one huge jump?'

'That is theoretically possible,' Fur said. 'But in practice it is dangerous. Gravity affects each hyperjump. That's why we have moved away from Globar 92 for so long before making our first jump. We needed to get away from the sun that the asteroid circles. If we had tried to make a jump as soon as we left the asteroid, there would be no predicting where we would end up.'

'Could we have materialised inside a star?' Adam asked.

Fur smiled. 'It's possible, but unlikely. Most of space is extremely empty. Most probably we would have just ended up lost.'

'But each time you make a jump,' Watch said, 'you recalculate what your next jump will be based on the gravitational influences in the immediate area?'

'Exactly,' Fur said, reaching for his controls. 'Now get ready, we are about to make the first jump. You might feel a moment of disorientation.'

'I feel that way most of the time,' Watch muttered.

Fur pushed a button and the stars outside suddenly rushed toward them at a dizzy speed. Then they vanished, and there was a moment of utter blackness, so deep Adam wasn't even sure if he was still alive. Just as quickly, the stars returned, but now they were not nearly as bright. Fur explained that they were now closer to the edge of the galaxy, where the stars were not as dense.

'Tallas 4 is not far from here,' Fur said. 'The Kasters like to hide in places far from the beaten tracks. Still, we will have to make another two jumps to reach the moon.'

'Are they ugly creatures?' Adam asked seriously.

'Not as ugly as human beings, if that's what you mean,' Fur laughed. 'Ugly is a relative term. Why, when you first met me I bet you thought I was ugly.'

'No offence but I still do,' Watch said.

Fur stopped laughing. 'I'll have you know I have had many dates with women from your planet and most of them were happy to get to know me.'

'Where did you meet these women?' Adam asked.

'At Hallowe'en parties.'

'It figures,' Watch muttered.

'And you just invited them over to your spaceship?' Adam asked.

'Sure,' Fur said. 'I use that exact line. Works like a wonder.'

'Why do you call your ship the *Fruitfly*?' Watch asked. 'On Earth that would be considered a demeaning title.'

Fur was offended. 'On my home world fruit-flies are considered quite a delicacy.'

Adam was horrified. 'You mean you eat flies. Yuck!'

'They don't taste bad when you chase them down with a Coke,' Fur said, his skilful hands working the controls. 'Prepare for another jump. I am almost ready.'

Over the next thirty minutes they made two more quick hyperjumps. Finally the large, red, gaseous planet around which Tallas 4 orbited came into view. Yet they knew it was large only because Fur said it was. They were still so far from it that it looked smaller than the Moon as seen from Earth.

'But Tallas itself is ten times larger than your Jupiter,' Fur explained as he turned the ship toward the planet and switched on the gravity drive that powered it through normal space.

'How long will it take to get there?' Adam asked.

'Ten hours,' Fur said.

'We can't jump the remainder of the distance?' Watch asked.

'No, for two reasons,' Fur said. 'It is too short a distance and in either case the force field surrounding Tallas would cause us to explode when we attempted to exit hyperspace.'

'Have you installed the Kaster force field we lent you?' Watch asked.

'Yes, but I don't want to use it to get through the planet's force field,' Fur said. 'I don't know if it's strong enough, and the Kaster watch the perimeter of this system closely. What I prefer to do is attach my ship to a small asteroid that flies near the Tallas defence field. If we use the *Fruitfly*'s engines carefully, we should be able alter the orbit of the asteroid slightly and fly close to Tallas without setting off any alarms. This system is thick with asteroids and we'll just be another big rock flying by.'

'That's a clever scheme,' Watch said, impressed.

Fur smiled. 'Do you still think I'm so ugly, Watch?'

'You would look fine after getting a deep tan, a thick wig, and a pair of coloured contact lenses,' Watch said.

'But will we have to break free of the asteroid to get to the moon?' Adam asked.

'Yes,' Fur said. 'Only then will we turn on the force field, and make ourselves invisible. The force field draws a lot of energy – we can't keep it on too long.'

'How are we going to blow up their computers?' Watch asked.

'We're not going to blow them up,' fur said.

'But we have to erase those debt records,' Adam protested.

'There is no way we can use heavy fire power around this moon and not be destroyed,' Fur said. 'We would be spotted in a moment. My plan is to sneak onto the surface of the moon, find a terminal, and hopefully erase your friend's names from the computers. Kaster systems are always interlinked. Any terminal should give us access to all their records.'

'And I suppose we can wear lizard make-up so that no one notices us?' Watch said sarcastically.

Fur was offended. 'I have thought of that. Not

everyone who works on Tallas 4 is a Kaster. They have off-world help. That's what we'll be.'

'It sounds like a good plan to me,' Adam said, trying to be supportive.

Fur took a while to find a suitable asteroid, one that was heading the right way and one that was bumpy enough to hide their small ship. They actually set down on the backside of the asteroid, and for a long time they couldn't see the red planet Tallas or its four moons. But during that time Fur carefully applied the power of the ship's engines to the rear of the asteroid.

'This far out we only have to change its course slightly to cause it to fly inside the perimeter of the force field,' he explained.

'Could the force field destroy the asteroid?' Watch asked.

'The asteroid should be able to absorb the energy, and save us the shock. As soon as we're through, we'll race towards Tallas 4.'

Fur almost proved to be an optimist. Many hours later, as the asteroid finally began to contact the Kaster force field, their own ship began to shake violently. It felt as if the surface of the asteroid where they had anchored was ready to explode. A wave of shimmering blue energy glittered in the space all around them. Adam hung on to his seat for dear life.

'This is a rough ride!' he shouted over the noise.

Fur laughed heartily. 'This is nothing!'

The rollercoaster ride stopped a minute later. They were through the main force field. Yet they were still far from the moon, although for the first time they were able to see it; a dull orange-coloured globe that looked both cold and uninviting. Fur continued to work the controls.

'We are turning on our invisibility cloak now,' he said.

The view outside changed only slightly. It was as if a thin sheet of hazy material were placed over the starry sky, dulling it but not blocking it out. Fur fired the *Fruitfly*'s gravity engines and slowly they lifted off the asteroid. The feeling of slow motion may have been only an illusion. Quickly enough, the dull orange moon began to grow in size. Everything seemed to be going according to plan, when suddenly there was a massive explosion behind them. They did not hear it – because they were in the vacuum of space which does not transmit sound waves – but they saw it. The explosion was blinding.

'What was that?' Adam gasped.

Fur sounded worried. 'The asteroid. They fired on it.'

'But why shoot at a rock?' Watch asked.

'Probably because they thought someone was using it for the very purpose we just used it for,' Fur said. 'To get by the force field. If we hadn't taken off when we did we would be dead now.' He paused. 'I told you this was a risky mission.'

'Risk is our middle name,' Adam said proudly.

'I don't have a middle name,' Watch said. 'I can hardly remember my last name.'

'They will be alert now,' Fur said. 'Our only hope is that they assume we perished in the explosion.'

'How come they can't penetrate their own cloaking device?' Watch asked.

'They can if they know where to look,' Fur said. 'But they will probably not look for anyone trying to land on Tallas 4.'

'Why not?' Adam said. 'Because of the food?'

'Because no one would be that stupid,' Fur said grimly.

The orange moon continued to grow outside the viewscreen. Soon it dominated the sky, and Fur's hands were glued to the controls. He passed over what looked like a highly-advanced city, but shook his head when Watch asked if the computers could be located there.

'We will never find the computers themselves,' Fur said. 'They could be anywhere. We just need one terminal to tap in to.'

'Then why don't you just land anywhere?' Watch asked.

Obviously the tension was getting to Fur.

'Why don't you just sit quietly and let me do the flying, OK?' he snapped.

'I was just trying to make conversation,' Watch muttered.

Fur dropped down low a few minutes later. For a moment it seemed they would crash, he was coming in so swiftly. But at the last second he pulled up, and Adam felt his stomach go down to the floor. The orange terrain was now a blur. There were canyons, there were tall buildings. Moving so fast it was hard to tell one from the other. But just as quickly, Fur brought them to a halt in a dark place where they could see literally nothing.

'Where are we?' Adam gasped.

'In somebody's garage,' Fur said. 'I spotted it on

my instruments. They left it open and hopefully they're not home right now.'

'You mean, we just landed in somebody's house?' Watch asked.

'Why not?' Fur asked. 'All the houses here will have a terminal.' He stood up from his chair. 'Let's hurry, we won't have long before we're spotted.'

Of course the home Fur had chosen was not empty. Two irritated crocodile creatures rushed at them the moment they stepped inside the Kaster home. Watch had to draw his laser pistol and stun them. Yet the Kaster creatures continued to flap their tails even in unconsciousness. Fur stepped over them nonchalantly.

'You can say what you want about them,' Fur said. 'But they are neat housekeepers.'

The home was in fact gorgeous, filled with towering rooms, frequent waterfalls, dark pools. It seemed the Kasters liked to spend half their time in water, like crocodiles on Earth.

Fur found a computer terminal in what appeared to be a bedroom and sat down. He turned the machine on and slipped what looked like a high-tech floppy disk in a side panel. The computer screen and the keyboard were much larger and complex than similar human components. Fur explained as he worked.

'The software I have inserted into their system was written by a form of bacteria on Demavon 123. They are really smart bugs – everyone goes to them for the latest computer games. This program will trace back to the Kaster's main computers. The program is great at getting into supposedly impenetrable files.'

'We could use that kind of bacteria on Earth,' Watch said. 'Our computer games are getting boring.'

'They tried to visit your world once,' Fur said. 'But they just ended up giving a New York cab-driver a chest cold. He went to the doctor and got a shot of penicillin and that wiped out the whole Demavon 123 expedition.' Fur stopped and laughed. 'I bet the cab-driver didn't realise what kind of royalties he gave up with that one shot. The bugs could have taught him how to program his yellow cab to make hyperjumps.'

'It is upon such small and insignificant incidents that the destinies of worlds turn,' Watch observed.

Fur let out a sound of joy. 'I am in their records!

Quick, how do you spell Sally and Cindy's full names?'

'Sally is officially Sara Wilcox,' Adam said. 'That's Sara without an H. Cindy is Cynthia Makey. Do you need help with any of those spellings?'

'No,' Fur said, still excited. 'I'm calling up their records now. And in a few seconds I should be able to erase them from the system by putting in another Demavon 123 program designed for just such a purpose. Then we can be out of here and on our way to Amacron 37 with a clean slate for your friends in hand.'

'Both Adam and I actually have a little debt as well,' Watch said.

Fur nodded. 'I suspected as much. How do you spell your last name, Watch?'

'I don't think even the Kasters know that,' Adam muttered.

Five minutes later Fur was not so confident. He had put in the bacteria's other program and become ensnared in a complex web of information he couldn't extricate himself from. It was only after a few minutes of fighting with the computer that realisation struck and Fur leaped to his feet.

'They must be on to us,' he exclaimed. 'They are just feeding me this garbage to make me think I am getting closer to getting rid of the records. But it's hopeless, we have to get out of here.' He turned in the direction they had entered. Adam grabbed his arm, stopping him.

'But we have come so far,' Adam pleaded. 'We can't quit now.'

Fur brushed off his hand. 'Don't you see, Adam, they are tracking us this very moment, back to this terminal. If we don't get off this moon in the next few seconds we will all end up on a slave planet.' Fur suddenly stopped. There was a banging outside. 'What was that noise?'

'Sounded like a gang of Kaster police pounding on the front door,' Watch said.

Fur stuck out his hand. 'Give me your laser pistol.'

'What will you trade me in return?' Watch asked.

'Our lives,' Adam said. 'Just give it to him. What are you going to do, Fur?'

Fur grabbed the weapon from Watch and began to fiddle with the controls. 'This can be set to overload. When it does it makes a respectable blast.' He stalked toward the door to the bedroom. 'When you hear the explosion, run for the ship. Don't look left or right, just keep running.' Fur opened the door. 'It's time to show the Kaster cops what your human "trick or treat" means.'

Adam and Watch looked at each other.

'How do we get into situations like this?' Adam said.

'We keep poor company,' Watch replied.

'Sally?'

'Sally is dangerous,' Watch said. 'She's worse than the Kasters.'

'But she does make our lives more exciting.'

'That is true,' Watch agreed.

There was a massive explosion. It was so powerful, so deafening, that Adam and Watch were sure Fur had perished trying to stop the Kasters. But they remembered his last instruction, to run for his ship no matter what, and that's what they did. But they had to run through smoke and fire to get there. They were more than a little relieved to find Fur already at the controls of the *Fruitfly*.

'What happened?' Adam gasped.

Fur grinned. 'I answered the door and politely asked them what they wanted. They didn't even reply. They immediately opened fire.' He added, 'I didn't tell you guys that I had removed the force field generator and carried it into the house in my pocket. Their laser beams bounced back on them and caused their whole load of weapons to explode.'

'You carried the force field on your own body so that at least you would be safe,' Watch said.

'Hey,' Fur said. 'I'm the only one here who can fly this ship. That makes me the most valuable person. Anyway, I have hooked the generator back up to the ship.' Fur nodded at the mess outside the forward viewing screen. 'We're going to need it like we never needed it before. Especially in the next two minutes.'

'If we fly into orbit they'll just blow us out of the sky,' Adam said as Fur started the ship's engines. Fur's hands flew over the controls.

'We're not going to stay around long enough for them to take aim,' Fur said.

'You're going to hyperjump as soon as we're in space,' Watch said, excited at the prospect.

'Exactly,' Fur said. 'Hold on.'

'But you said such a jump is uncontrollable!' Adam shouted as he was pressed back into his seat by the force of the acceleration. They roared out of what was left of the Kaster garage. The haunting orange sky loomed above them. But very quickly it began to darken, as they ploughed beyond the atmosphere and into space.

'Better an uncontrollable jump than certain death!' Fur yelled back. He glanced above as they broke completely free of the atmosphere. Mixed in the stars, there were three Kaster warships already rushing towards them. 'Prepare to jump!'

'But we still need to get to Amacron 37!' Adam yelled. 'We have to rescue the girls!'

'We rescue ourselves first!' Fur yelled.

And with that they jumped into hyperspace.

With no idea where they would end up.

# Nine

Sally stood in Teeh's office and wondered what she was supposed to tell the Kaster boss. So intent had she been on just getting to the head of the compound's power, she had not planned how she was going to get out of the office. Teeh, still slobbering and still wearing his cheap sunglasses, sat down opposite her. There was no other chair and he didn't offer to get her one. The crocodile boss put his scaly feet up on his dirty desk and looked at her as if she had better have a good reason for requesting a private audience.

'Well?' he said. 'Where are your friends?'

Sally swallowed. 'They're not here.'

'I know they're not here. Do I look stupid or what? Where are they?'

'They're on their way here,' she said.

'What are you talking about?'

'Has the Collector you sent to fetch us returned?'

'I ask the questions here!' Teeh paused. 'No. It hasn't.'

'Adam and Watch destroyed it.'

Teeh sat up straight. 'How do you know this?'

Sally felt herself getting in the mood to tell some really great lies.

It was a special feeling of wonderful power.

'I know them. They're powerful young men. At this very moment they have allied themselves with other powerful beings and they are on their way here to rescue Cindy and me.'

Teeh snorted. 'You're dreaming. No one tries to rescue anyone from Amacron 37. It's a dust-bowl – hardly anyone can find this place.'

'Then where is your Collector?' Sally asked.

Teeh scratched his scaly head. 'Well, I don't rightly know. I suppose it is possible your friends got the upper hand with him. What is it they ordered anyway?'

'Watch ordered a laser pistol and a personal force field generator.' Sally added, 'He also got himself a telescope.'

Teeh frowned. 'We have to stop offering those

personal force-field generators. We lose more Collectors that way.' He paused and studied her. 'Why are you telling me all this?'

'I told you, I want to get ahead. And I don't mind betraying my friends to do it. I tell you seriously, they are on their way here this very minute. If you don't take care, they will remove you as boss of this slave planet.'

'Who are the powerful beings they have made friends with?'

Sally darkened her expression. 'The Treeboards.'

'I haven't heard of them. What sector are they from?'

'They don't even come from this galaxy. They're from a black hole at the edge of the universe. They're an ancient race. They were highly evolved when your race and mine were bacteria swimming in primeval mud. They have powers we can't even dream of.'

'Then what would they want with your friends?'

Sally spoke in wicked whispers. 'They have allied themselves with Adam and Watch because they have a common goal. You see, the Treeboards have an ancient and undying hatred for ugly lizards like . . . for reptilian super-races like your own.

Adam and Watch have stolen your Collector's transporter. Now they have an easy map that leads straight here, and the evil Treeboards want to come along for the ride, to destroy you when they see you. To destroy all Kasters, wherever they may be.' Sally paused for effect. 'The shield you have erected around Amacron 37 will not stop them. It won't even come close.'

Teeh appeared unsure of himself. 'This story sounds outlandish. Can you prove that these Treeboards even exist?'

'Yes. I spent time with them, on a lost moon circling a dead quasar, ten billion light years from here. They taught me many of their secrets, and I can show you some of those secrets now. I can teach you how to strengthen the force field that surrounds this planet so that even the Treeboards – even Watch and Adam – cannot get through it with their fleet of super tachyon spaceships.'

Teeh raised an eyebrow. 'What are those?'

'Highly-developed vessels that you'll never see in a Collector's Christmas catalogue. Listen to me, Teeh, please, I am the only one that can save you. If you will just give me a few minutes with your computer, I can prove it to you.'

Teeh considered. 'What do you want in return for this help?'

'You must erase my Wishing Stone debt.'

'What about the debt of your friend, Cindy?'

Sally waved her hand. 'She is of no concern to me. She can rot here for the rest of eternity for all I care.'

Teeh grinned. She had hit the right nerve. He was now convinced.

'Spoken like a true Kaster,' he said. 'Are you sure you don't have reptilian blood in your veins, Sally?'

'My grandmother always used to say my grandfather was a snake. I never met him myself but I heard the stories. He was your kind of man, Teeh. And I am your girl. Where's your computer?'

Teeh stood and moved toward an elaborate control panel. 'You understand while you work on my computer I have to stand and supervise?'

Sally stood and followed him to the computer. It looked like a bunch of lights and buttons to her. She wished Watch was with her now.

'Naturally,' she said. 'It is my hope that I can teach you a few things.' She added, 'I mean that with all due respect, of course.'

'Of course,' Teeh said, in a good mood, for him.

'You are familiar with my operating system? The famous Kaster double matrix algorithm TEC dot software?'

Sally waved her hand as she sat down in front of the massive computer. 'I learned about that when I was in first grade. It is an extremely primitive system when compared to what the Treeboards use.' Sally touched the keyboards and then paused. 'I need an electric stick.'

'What?'

'One of those sticks that your primitive robots carry. I need one.'

'What for?'

'I am going to link it into your computer system so that this whole planet will be transformed into one cosmic-sized electric stick which will be capable of repelling the super tachyon fleet that races toward this planet at this very instant.' Sally had to pause to catch her breath. 'Do you have one in your desk?'

Teeh turned back to his desk. 'I believe so. But frankly this kind of technology confuses me. I have never seen anything like it.'

'Neither have I,' whispered Sally.

'What?'

'Nothing. Everything will quickly become clear. The power of your protective shield will change beyond your wildest dreams. With this technology, you will be the single most power Kaster in this section of the galaxy.'

Teeh found an electric stick in one of his drawers. 'I have not had the advantage of your obviously extensive education. How long will it take me to comprehend the Treeboard technology?'

'A sly lizard like . . . I mean, a brilliant Kaster like you – you will know more than I do before we both leave this room.' She stuck out her hand and took the electric stick. 'Now I just need to know one other thing.'

Teeh stood nearby. 'What?'

'Where does this computer plug in?'

'What do you mean?'

'Its power source. Where does it draw its power from?'

Teeh nodded to a black box to the side of the control panel. 'From there. Do you need more power? I can have extra cables brought in.'

'Maybe. Open the power box. Let me study it.'

Teeh did so. It looked much like a fuse box back home.

Sally turned on the electric stick and got up. 'Stand aside, Teeh.'

He did as she requested but a flicker of doubt crossed his face.

'What are you doing?' he asked.

'Changing the polarity of the situation.' Sally rammed the tip of the electric stick into the black box. The thing literally exploded in sparks. She knew immediately that the damage was enough to knock out the force field and all the robots. She turned the stick on Teeh and smiled wickedly up at his blustering expression. 'I am changing everything,' she said.

He was enraged. 'You will pay for this!'

'Wrong! We're through paying!'

And with that Sally stuck the electric stick up his fat snout.

Tech turned a deeper green than normal and fainted.

Sally stepped on his cheap sunglasses as she fled the room.

# *Ten*

They came out of hyperspace in the centre of the galaxy. There were so many stars in the sky that it was hard to find any black space. Fur quickly handed them each a pair of thick sunglasses. Watch stared out of the viewing screen, enthralled.

'I'll never see anything like this in my telescope,' he said.

'If we don't get out of here quickly we won't be seeing, period,' Fur said.

'Why not?' Adam asked.

'There are tremendous levels of radiation at the galactic core,' Fur explained. 'Our force field is keeping them at bay for the moment but that situation will not last. The first thing this kind of radiation burns is the optic nerves.'

'Can we make another hyperjump so close

to all these stars?' Watch asked.

Fur was grim. 'We have no choice. But it could tear us apart.'

'We will go out in a blaze of glory,' Watch said, still staring at the stars.

'What glory?' Adam asked. 'We failed in our quest. We weren't able to destroy the records on Tallas 4. Our debts will last for ever. We will never be free of them.'

'Isn't there a saying on your world?' Fur said as he worked the controls. 'It ain't over till it's over? That's my motto. Hold on, we're going to make another jump, and I can guarantee this one will be rough.'

They leaped into hyperspace, and this jump was different from the others. Not really rough, but it seemed as if the period of blackness lasted for ever. During the time Adam wondered if that was not literally the case, if they would not be trapped for eternity outside of normal space and time. But finally the stars reappeared. Fur checked his navigation computer.

'I know where we are!' he exclaimed.

'Where?' asked Adam.

'In the Beta quadrant. We're not far from

Amacron 37.' He paused. 'Are you sure you still want to go there? We'll never get through their force fields. Slave planets are strictly off limits.'

'We have to try,' Adam said.

'But we can always try later,' Watch said.

'Watch!' Adam complained. 'I'm disappointed in you.'

'I would rather live with your disappointment than die in a Kaster force field,' Watch replied. But then he paused and gave it some thought. 'But I suppose we might succeed in the end. We usually do.' He nodded to Fur. 'Plot a hyperjump for Amacron 37.'

'And may the Force be with us,' Adam said.

'*Star Wars*,' Fur quipped. 'Great movie.'

A few minutes later they were again flying through hyperspace.

When Sally ran from Teeh's office, she saw immediately that her plan had worked. The robot guards were all standing immobilised. Yet her plan had its limits, as Cindy had pointed out. There was no where to go except into the desert.

Cindy and Hironee came out of the work warehouse as Sally ran over. The other slaves were still inside, casting hesitant looks in their direction, but with nothing else to do now that the power was off all over the compound.

'What's happened?' Hironee asked.

'I disabled the computer,' Sally said. 'That means that the force field is down for the time being. We have to get out of here before it comes back on-line.'

'But what happened to Teeh?' Cindy asked.

'He's taking a nap,' Sally said.

'A nap?' Hironee said, puzzled.

'With an electric toothpick up his nose. Look, we can talk about this once we're deep in the desert and clear of the force field.'

Cindy nodded. 'I'll get us water bottles, a pack of supplies.' She dashed off to collect the stuff. For the moment Sally was left alone with Hironee, although a robot stood perfectly still nearby, caught in mid-stride by the drop in power. Sally was surprised to see Hironee was not excited and asked her what was the matter. The green-faced girl answered with her head down.

'We can't go into the desert,' she said softly. 'Charles went into the desert and he died.'

Sally put a hand on her shoulder. 'Charles did not knock out the robots like we have. They were the ones who hunted him down and killed him. Also, Charles was alone. In the desert we can help each other.' Sally paused. 'Something else is bothering you.'

Hironee nodded weakly. 'I hate this place. I've told you how much I hate it. But I've been here half my life. It's home to me now. I know that sounds silly but I'm afraid to leave it.' She stopped and there were tears in her eyes. 'You and Cindy had better leave without me.'

'Nonsense. We will never do that.' Sally gave her a hug and then gestured to the barren landscape. 'This is no home for a person like you. Try to remember what Zanath was like – the blue water, the green islands, the warm yellow sun in the clear sky. That's your home, Hironee, and if you come with us you might see it again soon. But I'm not promising you will. Maybe you will die in the desert like Charles. That's a definite possibility. But you have to know deep inside that it's better to die free than live as a slave.'

Hironee smiled at the words. 'You never told me, Sally, that you were such a motivational speaker.'

Sally laughed. 'My talents are endless.' She turned toward the building where Cindy had disappeared. 'Let's take what supplies we can carry and let's get out of here before Mr Lizard Breath wakes up.'

They came out of hyperspace much closer to Amacron 37 than they had been to the other worlds when they finished making their jumps. Fur explained that he had intentionally cut it close so that the Kasters would have less time to spot them.

'But we can circle around the planet until they shoot us down if we're hoping to get into their slave compounds,' he said gloomily as they raced toward the desert planet, a purple sun hanging in the sky off to their right.

'Are the force fields just around the slave compounds?' Watch asked.

'Usually,' Fur said. 'There's no point in protecting all of a planet like this. It's mostly dust and sand. The Kasters usually concentrate their energy where it's most needed. But that allows them to erect an even stronger force field in a small area. Don't fool yourself, this place is more protected than Tallas 4 was.'

'Where we were far from a huge success,' Watch observed.

'Is there no way to get through the force fields?' Adam asked, feeling frustrated.

'We can try,' Fur said. 'We can turn the generator Watch has lent me up to full power and try to smash through. But there is an excellent chance we will explode.'

'Better not risk it,' Watch said, having second thoughts.

'We have to give it a try,' Adam said.

Fur stared at him. 'These two girls must be pretty special.'

'One of them is,' Watch said. 'The other is just unusual.'

'They are our friends,' Adam said. 'That's what matters.'

Fur was wistful. 'I wish I had friends as loyal as you two.' He added, 'Or at least as loyal as you, Adam.' Something on the control panel caught his eye. He pushed a couple of buttons, seemingly rechecking his readings. 'This is odd.'

'What is it?' Adam asked.

'The southernmost compound on Amacron 37 – their force field is shut down. Not only that, but there are three life-signs heading away from the compound, heading deep into the desert.'

'It must be the girls!' Adam exclaimed.

'I thought there were only two of them,' Fur said.

'They make friends fast,' Watch said. 'At least Cindy does.'

Something else on the control panel caught Fur's eye. But rather than trying to ascertain exactly what his instruments were showing, he leaned his head back and stared up at the window on the ceiling of the control room. Adam and Watch did likewise, in time to see a fleet of warships materialise in normal space. Clearly the ships had just completed a jump through hyperspace. They were grey in colour, long and sleek, with red fins and smouldering weapon-ports.

'The Kaster,' Fur said softly, stunned. 'They must have followed us here from Tallas 4.'

'They could trace us through hyperspace?' Watched asked.

Fur shook his head. 'No. But they didn't have to. They figured we were coming here because we were trying to erase records related to Amacron 37.'

'Do we have to surrender?' Adam asked.

Fur was grim. 'The Kaster do not take prisoners in a situation like this.'

100

'Then we must try to jump into hyperspace again,' Watch said.

'No,' Adam said. 'We have to get the girls first.'

'If we land, we will be completely helpless,' Fur said. 'They will destroy us at their leisure. I agree with Watch. We must try to escape.' Fur went to push the button that would launch them into hyperspace. But Adam stopped him by putting a hand on his arm.

'The girls have knocked out the Amacron 37 force field when you said that was impossible,' Adam said. 'They are out in the desert, fighting for their lives, for freedom. How can we just abandon them when they have fought so hard and we are so close to them?'

Watch spoke up. 'Adam has a point. Even I would feel guilty leaving them at this point.'

Fur studied his instruments. 'They are not alone in the desert. A force of robots is now on their tail.' He looked at them. 'If we land we will have enemies on all sides.'

Adam didn't hesitate. 'Land. We either save them or else we all die together.'

Watch patted Fur on the back and tried to

reassure the trader. 'We're all from Spooksville. We have an excellent track record in hopeless situations.'

Fur sighed. 'I don't.'

# Eleven

Hironee saw the *Fruitfly* first. They were trudging around a massive sand-dune when it appeared in the sky above them. Burning with the flames of re-entry, heading straight for them like a meteor shot out of a stellar cannon.

'Look!' Hironee shouted.

Sally and Cindy almost fell over when they saw the ship.

'Is it a Kaster vessel?' Sally asked, fully expecting the answer to be yes.

Hironee squinted. 'No, I don't think so. It looks more like a trader ship.'

Sally looked at Cindy. 'It could be Adam and Watch.'

Cindy nodded anxiously. 'Hope so.'

But just then all hope seemed to fade. The fleet

of Kaster warships – chasing the trader vessel – became visible at the same time that Teeh and his robots rounded the sand-dune behind the girls. The Kaster warships had torpedo tubes on both sides that glowed with a wicked red light. Teeh had a small fleet of powerful ground vehicles that resembled open-air tanks. Both Kaster groups seemed to be in the middle of taking aim. Yet perhaps Teeh, seeing the ships overhead, warned them off. The slimy boss probably didn't want to get blasted with the humans. Overhead the ships suddenly veered off to the side. Yet they did not fly away, rather they began to swoop in at a low altitude.

In the meantime the trader ship landed nearby.

Adam and Watch and a ghost character with a bald head and a cigar in his mouth jumped out. The girls ran to the boys and embraced them.

'Are we glad to see you!' Cindy exclaimed, giving Adam a big hug.

'We are happy to see you!' Adam said, hugging her back.

'I was the one who disabled the Kaster force field,' Sally said quickly.

'I was the one who blew up the Kaster house,'

Fur said, watching both the approaching land army and the hovering warships. 'But it looks like we both only managed to anger the wrong people.'

'And who may I ask are you?' Sally asked suspiciously.

Fur bowed. 'I am Fur and I am here to rescue you.' He glanced at Watch. 'This must be the unusual one.'

'I knew you would spot her immediately,' Watch said.

'I will have you know that it was I who said you were on your way here to rescue us,' Sally said. 'While Cindy here was ready to bury you, as usual I might add.'

Fur gestured to the approaching armoured car, which carried several robots and the grand master of slobbers himself – Kaster boss Teeh. His snout looked swollen and sore. He held a black laser rifle in his two stubby arms.

'I think we might all be buried in a few minutes,' Fur said.

Teeh parked only a few metres away and his robots immediately jumped from the armoured vehicle and surrounded them on all sides, pointing mean-looking lasers at their heads. Teeh likewise approached and he did not look in a good mood. Although he carried a weapon, his free hand kept moving to his bruised snout. He went straight to Sally and glared at her.

'I am going to peel you alive!' he swore. 'I will swallow your flesh before your very eyes! You will die with your own screams in your ears!'

Sally spoke sweetly. 'Did the Treeboards hurt your nose, Mr Teeh?'

Teeh growled. 'There are no Treeboards!'

'Of course there are,' Watch said. 'All boards come from trees.'

'I know that!' Teeh said. 'Do I look stupid or something? I . . .'

'You do look stupid,' Cindy interrupted, surprising them all. She just shrugged when they stared at her. 'He looks like a stupid crocodile from a dirty swamp. What can I say?'

Teeh was not amused. 'You will pay for that!'

Sally snorted. 'I told you, we're through paying. If you're going to kill us, kill us now and get it over with. We're not afraid to die.'

'I would like to mention that Sally does not speak for all of us,' Watch said.

'I would like to second that,' Fur said.

Just then one of the Kaster warships settled to the ground behind *Fruitfly*. The vessel was massive, powerful; it cast a steaming shadow over the entire area. An official-looking Kaster captain with a host of lizard guards approached, making a mess of the sand-dune with their swishing tails. The captain clearly outranked Teeh, who quickly bowed to the commander of the warship.

'Captain Thorath,' Teeh said. 'A pleasure. What brings you to Amacron 37?'

Captain Thorath pointed a scaly finger at Fur. 'This trader invaded Tallas 4 and tried to wipe out several debt records from our computer files. I am here to arrest him and bring him back to Tallas 4 for immediate trial and execution.'

'At least you get a trial,' Watch said to Fur.

'It sounds like I will have trouble finding an impartial jury,' Fur said.

'What about these other two humans?' Teeh asked Captain Thorath, pointing to Adam and Watch. Captain Thorath did not answer immediately. He seemed to be caught off guard by the question. He studied Adam and Watch, seemingly trying to figure out a problem that was bothering him.

'Which one of you is Adam?' he asked finally.

'I am,' Adam said.

'Tell him what a slob he is,' Sally said in his ear. 'Don't let him intimidate you.'

'Shh,' Adam cautioned.

Captain Thorath stepped closer to Adam. The commander appeared to be still puzzled over what to do next, what to say, 'You made an unusual wish with one of our stones,' he said finally.

'I wished for galactic peace,' Adam said.

'You did?' Fur said with interest.

'Yes,' Adam said with a sad note in his voice. He gestured to the warships, the armed robots that continued to point at them with their weapons. "But it doesn't look like my wish will be granted any time soon.'

'But it must be granted,' Fur said with excitement in his tone.

Captain Thorath quickly held up a scaly hand. 'We need not go into that right now,' he said.

Fur stepped forward. 'But you know the rules, Commander. The whole galaxy knows them.' Fur turned back to Adam. 'Tell me, was your wish on the same order as the others?'

'This is nonsense,' Teeh interrupted, speaking to

the warship commander. 'Let's kill them all now and eat their skins.'

'His wish was on the same order,' Sally said to Fur. 'The Collector stated that fact.'

Fur smiled and turned to Captain Thorath. 'Then you cannot collect on any of their wishes. Not until every wish on the order has been granted. Those are your own rules written by your own senate.'

'We don't grant the wishes until the debts have been paid off,' Teeh said bitterly.

Fur shook his head. 'Your commander knows better. You grant the wishes, then come to collect the debts, then give the stuff back when the debts have been paid off.' He added with bitterness, 'Of course you never really have to give anything away. All your slaves die before they get back what they wished for.'

'As well they should,' Teeh said. 'Do we look like we're stupid? We . . .'

'Shut up, Teeh,' Captain Thorath told the slave boss. He spoke to the gang. 'It is true what your trader friend says. We cannot legally collect on your debts until all the wishes on the same order have been fulfilled. But Adam, because your wish is so

109

unusual, we doubt if we will ever be able to grant it.' He paused. 'For that reason we would prefer you make another wish. Something simple, easy to make in our factories.'

'But if I do that we will all end up as slaves,' Adam said.

Captain Thorath sighed. 'I was afraid you would say that.' He spread his hands. 'Then what should we do? I am open to suggestions.'

Fur spoke to the gang. 'Don't do anything. Let the wish for galactic peace remain. Then the Kaster will be obliged to fulfil it before they can come after you again. And that wish will never be granted, especially by the Kaster. They are always at war with somebody.'

'But we can't let these humans go!' Teeh broke in. 'This one here electrocuted my snout!'

'Good for her,' Captain Thorath muttered, thinking, his gaze momentarily far away. Finally he turned back to the gang. 'Very well, a rule is a rule, and we shouldn't be breaking our own if we expect others to listen to them.' He drew in a deep breath. 'You are not obliged to pay your debts until all the wishes on your order have been fulfilled.'

'Which in practice means you won't ever have to pay them,' Fur said.

'Do we get to keep the things we wished for?' Sally asked.

Captain Thorath hesitated, 'Yes.'

Sally squealed with delight. 'I knew what I was doing all along! I'm rich!'

But Captain Thorath pointed at Fur and Hironee. 'But this trader is coming back to Tallas 4 with me, to be tried and executed. And Teeh, you can do what you wish with this disobedient slave.'

'I will eat her flesh in front of her eyes!' Teeh exclaimed.

Hironee cowered. 'No.'

'Get over the flesh thing already,' Sally muttered. She put her arm around Hironee's shoulders and spoke to the commander. 'You can't hurt our friend. We won't let you.'

Fur looked anxiously around. 'Why isn't anyone hugging me?'

Teeh gloated at Sally. 'We can do whatever we want with both of them.'

Adam took another step forward. 'Wait a second. Captain Thorath, between the four of us we wished for some pretty expensive items. We got money, a

111

laser pistol, a force-field generator, a new telescope, spring outfits. These things must have cost the Kaster a pretty penny.'

Captain Thorath studied him. 'What is your point, young man?'

'What if we give you these things back?' Adam said. 'And in exchange you let Hironee and Fur go?'

Sally took her arm of Hironee. 'Don't give my money back,' Sally whispered to Adam.

'I really like that telescope,' Watch said.

'Your proposition is an interesting one,' Captain Thorath said. 'A dead trader is of little use to us, and I am sure Teeh here has plenty of slaves to eat.' He paused. 'I will accept your offer to return all the goods, as long as you can all agree on the offer.'

'I agree,' Fur said.

'You don't count,' Sally snapped at him. 'I say we return everything except the money and Hironee gets to go free with us.'

'But Fur is our friend,' Adam protested.

'But we haven't known him that long,' Watch said.

Adam held up his hands. 'Wait a second! How

112

can we have galactic peace if we can't even have peace among ourselves? We're all friends here. We have to stick together like friends should. We either return everything and all go free or else we remain here and labour away until the end of our lives.' He paused for effect. 'What's it going to be?'

Watch shrugged. 'I already have a pretty good telescope at home.'

Sally hesitated. 'I suppose I will get rich anyway, either as a famous actress or a best-selling novelist.'

Adam smiled and offered his hand to Captain Thorath. 'It's a deal.'

Captain Thorath shook his hand and nodded. 'You continue to think big, Adam. The galaxy needs more people like you.'

Hironee turned to Sally. 'I get to return to Zanath?'

Sally hugged her. 'Yeah, and your ticket's costing me a couple of million. But don't let that bother you. I just mention it in passing.'

Fur beamed and puffed on his cigar. 'I can take you back to Zanath. Heck, I can take the rest of you back to Earth.' He turned towards his spaceship, and the rest of them followed. 'I've got to see this famous Spooksville. It sounds like a happening place.'

Sally glanced one last time at desolate Amacron 37 and turned up her nose.

'Yeah,' she said. 'At least it beats this place.'

## ABOUT THE AUTHOR

Christopher Pike was born in New York, but grew up in Los Angeles, where he still lives. Prior to becoming a writer he worked in a factory, painted houses and programmed computers. His hobbies include astronomy, meditating, running and making sure his books are prominently displayed in his local bookshop. As well as being a best-selling children's writer, he is also the author of three adult novels.

*If you enjoyed these stories you'll love
Christopher Pike's other Spooksville
Chillers . . .*

# Spooksville

## THE WICKED CAT

A tree falls down.
A house catches fire.
Bad things happen.

And the cat is always there, watching.
With its strange green eyes.

Then it begins to use its power
on Adam and his friends . . .

# *Spooksville*

## THE DEADLY PAST

Huge meat-eating lizards attack people.
Flying reptiles swoop down on chidlren.
Dinosaurs roam the woods.

Adam and his friends discover
a doorway from sixty million
years ago. Can they close it before
Spooksville is destroyed?

# *Spooksville*

## THE HIDDEN BEAST

The dragon will stop at nothing.
It will breathe fire and destroy
Spooksville.
It will burn children to ash.
All to find its treasure of gold and jewels.
How can Adam and his friends
end its reign of terror?

*Spooksville*

## *Spooksville*
# CHRISTOPHER PIKE

*All Hodder Children's books are available at your local bookshop, or can be ordered direct from the publisher. Just tick the titles you would like and complete the details below. Prices and availability are subject to change without prior notice.*

Please enclose a cheque or postal order made payable to *Bookpoint Ltd*, and send to: Hodder Children's Books, 39 Milton Park, Abingdon, OXON OX14 4TD, UK. Email Address: orders@bookpoint.co.uk

If you would prefer to pay by credit card, our call centre team would be delighted to take your order by telephone. Our direct line *01235 400414* (lines open 9.00 am–6.00 pm Monday to Saturday, 24 hour message answering service). Alternatively you can send a fax on *01235 400454*.

| TITLE | | FIRST NAME | | SURNAME | |
|---|---|---|---|---|---|

| ADDRESS | |
|---|---|
| | |
| | |
| | |

| DAYTIME TEL: | | POST CODE | |
|---|---|---|---|

If you would prefer to pay by credit card, please complete:
Please debit my Visa/Access/Diner's Card/American Express (delete as applicable) card no:

| | | | | | | | | | | | | | | | | | | |
|---|---|---|---|---|---|---|---|---|---|---|---|---|---|---|---|---|---|---|

Signature .......................................................................................................

Expiry Date: .................................................................................................

If you would NOT like to receive further information on our products please tick the box. ❏